WORLD IN REVERSE

Borgo Press Books by JOHN RUSSELL FEARN

1,000-Year Voyage: A Science Fiction Novel * *Anjani the Mighty: A Lost Race Novel* (Anjani #2) * *Black Maria, M.A.: A Classic Crime Novel* (Black Maria #1) * *Bury the Hatchet* * *A Case for Brutus Lloyd* * *The Crimson Rambler: A Crime Novel* * *Death in Silhouette* (Black Maria #5) * *Don't Touch Me: A Crime Novel* * *Dynasty of the Small: Classic Science Fiction Stories* * *The Empty Coffins: A Mystery of Horror* * *The Fourth Door: A Mystery Novel* * *From Afar: A Science Fiction Mystery* * *Fugitive of Time: A Classic Science Fiction Novel* * *The G-Bomb: A Science Fiction Novel* * *The Genial Dinosaur* (Herbert the Dinosaur #2) * *The Gold of Akada: A Jungle Adventure Novel* (Anjani #1) * *Here and Now: A Science Fiction Novel* * *Into the Unknown: A Science Fiction Tale* * *Last Conflict: Classic Science Fiction Stories* * *Legacy from Sirius: A Classic Science Fiction Novel* * *The Man from Hell: Classic Science Fiction Stories* * *The Man Who Was Not: A Crime Novel* * *Manton's World: A Classic Science Fiction Novel* * *Moon Magic: A Novel of Romance* (as Elizabeth Rutland) * *The Murdered Schoolgirl: A Classic Crime Novel* (Black Maria #2) * *One Remained Seated: A Classic Crime Novel* (Black Maria #3) * *One Way Out: A Crime Novel* (with Philip Harbottle) * *Pattern of Murder: A Classic Crime Novel* * *Reflected Glory: A Dr. Castle Classic Crime Novel* * *Robbery Without Violence: Two Science Fiction Crime Stories* * *Rule of the Brains: Classic Science Fiction Stories* * *Shattering Glass: A Crime Novel* * *The Silvered Cage: A Scientific Murder Mystery* * *Slaves of Ijax: A Science Fiction Novel* * *Something from Mercury: Classic Science Fiction Stories* * *The Space Warp: A Science Fiction Novel* * *A Thing of the Past* (Herbert the Dinosaur #1) * *Thy Arm Alone: A Classic Crime Novel* (Black Maria #4) * *The Time Trap: A Science Fiction Novel* * *Vision Sinister: A Scientific Detective Thriller* * *Voice of the Conqueror: A Classic Science Fiction Novel* * *What Happened to Hammond? A Scientific Mystery* * *Within That Room!: A Classic Crime Novel* * *World Without Chance*

THE GOLDEN AMAZON SAGA

1. *World Beneath Ice* * 2. *Lord of Atlantis* * 3. *Triangle of Power* * 4. *The Amethyst City* * 5. *Daughter of the Amazon* * 6. *Quorne Returns* * 7. *The Central Intelligence* * 8. *The Cosmic Crusaders* * 9. *Parasite Planet* * 10. *World Out of Step* * 11. *The Shadow People* * 12. *Kingpin Planet* * 13. *World in Reverse* * 14. *Dwellers in Darkness* * 15. *World in Duplicate* * 16. *Lords of Creation* * 17. *Duel with Colossus* * 18. *Standstill Planet* * 19. *Ghost World* * 20. *Earth Divided* * 21. *Chameleon Planet* (with Philip Harbottle)

WORLD IN REVERSE

THE GOLDEN AMAZON SAGA, BOOK THIRTEEN

JOHN RUSSELL FEARN

Edited by Philip Harbottle

THE BORGO PRESS
MMXIII

WORLD IN REVERSE

FIRST BORGO PRESS EDITION

Published by Wildside Press LLC

www.wildsidebooks.com

DEDICATION

To the Memory of Iris Weigh

CONTENTS

THE GOLDEN AMAZON

by Philip Harbottle

In 1943 British writer John Russell Fearn decided to quit writing for the American pulp science fiction magazines, and to concentrate instead on books for the English market. Within a very few years he became established as a leading novelist in several genres, not only science fiction, but also mystery and detective fiction, and westerns.

His first new SF novel, *The Golden Amazon*, was published by World's Work in April 1944. In this story, a little girl of three years of age is made the subject of an idealistic scientist's illegal glandular experiments. The scientist's dream is to end world wars by creating a woman devoid of the usual lusts and frailties of mankind, who upon reaching maturity would institute a benign scientific rule. But the apparently successful experiment has a flaw: it instills into the girl a hatred for all men, and a ruthless cruelty. Her supernatural scientific gifts enable her to master atomic power, and practically leads her to destroy the world. She breaks the will and strength of men, and elevates women to positions of wealth and power. She also discovers human synthesis, and by this means she is able to escape retribution when she is eventually overthrown. She is seen to collapse and die, a victim of consuming ketabolism, echoing the memorable finale of Rider Haggard's *She*. In actuality, it was only her synthetic image, and this paved the way for the *Golden Amazon Returns*, and further sequels

Fearn sold reprint rights in the first novel to the prestigious Canadian magazine, the Toronto *Star Weekly*. The magazine carried a special Comics Supplement, the centre section of which was a 'complete novel', published in newspaper format. Aimed at a general readership, the novels were written by the top popular novelists of the day, including John Dickson Carr, Ellery Queen, and P. G. Wodehouse. They sold hundreds of thousands of copies, and the novels were syndicated to several American newspapers in the Maine and New York areas. The Amazon novels enjoyed extraordinary popularity (especially with Canadian housewives), and ran for the next sixteen years following the appearance of the first novel in the March 3, 1945 issue, ending with Fearn's sudden death in September 1960, aged only fifty-two. His final two Amazon novels appeared posthumously.

During Fearn's lifetime, only the first six novels were published in British hardcover editions from the World's Work in England, after appearing in the *Star Weekly*. This was because the publishers discontinued their entire fiction line in 1954. However, the Amazon novels continued to appear in the *Star Weekly*, eventually notching up twenty-four titles.

Fearn had resold paperback rights to the Canadian publisher Harlequin Books, but after publishing only the first three titles, they stopped publishing SF and other genre fiction to concentrate on their famous Romances line.

Meanwhile, as early as 1949, Fearn had realized that the Amazon series had the potential to run indefinitely. This presented him with a problem, however. The 'origin story' of the Golden Amazon was conceived and actually set during the Second World War. Subsequent novels were written during the war and the immediate postwar period, and projected their stories only a few decades into the future.

He very astutely realized that to keep ahead of reality, he needed to move the Amazon *further* into the future—first into the outer solar system, and thence to the stars. So with the seventh novel, he introduced a new main character, Abna of Atlantis—someone as equally intelligent, and even stronger than herself. These dynamics provided him with an *interstellar* canvas, thus ensuring that the series would remain ahead of reality.

Fearn's strategy was a great success, and the Amazon novels retained their popularity, ending only with his tragically early death in 1960. By then he had written a further twenty Amazon novels, and made prelimi-nary notes for his next (which would later be written by Fearn's biographer, Philip Harbottle).

Long after Fearn's death, his entire Amazon series

would eventually see print from the pioneering US small press Gryphon Books in limited paperback editions, and later by the Canadian Battered Silicon Dispatch Box small press in their hardcover Omnibus series.

This new Borgo Press paperback series will be the first trade edition of all twenty-one of these later novels by Fearn, beginning with the seventh novel in the original series. First published in 1949 as *Conquest of the Amazon*, I have edited it slightly as *World Beneath Ice* (The Golden Amazon Saga, Book One) so that it can be read and enjoyed by new readers who may be totally unfamiliar with what had gone before. Subsequent novels have also been slightly edited for modern readers.

The publishers hope that this new series may create many more "fans of the Amazon." Meanwhile, any reader interested in seeking out the earlier six Golden Amazon novels will find that they are readily available on the internet, and in numerous earlier paperback and hardcover editions.

* * * * * * * * *

To date, readers can enjoy the following new Borgo Press editions:

Book One: *World Beneath Ice*

In destroying the threat of an alien invasion, the Golden Amazon had inadvertently caused a decline in the sun's heat, encasing Earth in an ice sheet that threatens to eliminate humanity. The Amazon encounters Abna, a descendant of Atlantis, stronger and even more scientifically advanced than she, and the ruler of an Atlantean colony still surviving in a protected environment on Jupiter. She refuses his offer of marriage, but agrees to form an alliance in order to restore the sun and save the Earth. One thing that Abna has not told the Amazon is that all the females of his race have been wiped out by a bacilli infection....

Book Two: *Lord of Atlantis*

A gigantic ridge of land rises from the Atlantic floor, causing massive tidal waves on either side of the ocean. Even stranger, both England and America are then assailed by an invasion of prehistoric monsters! A gigantic domed city rests on the newly risen plateau, whilst out in space an alien spacecraft orbits the Earth. Such are the mysteries and challenges facing the Golden Amazon, self-appointed governess of Earth, as she struggles to unravel the maze of mystery that was the deadly legacy of Atlantis!

Book Three: *Triangle of Power*

The marriage of Violet Ray Brant—better known as The Golden Amazon—and Abna of Atlantis should have ushered in an era of peace and scientific prosperity to the people of Earth. But an unexpected turn of events finds Abna betrayed and marooned on a satellite of Jupiter, and the Amazon flung far beyond the Solar System. With Earth's two protectors removed, the planet is now at the mercy of another Atlantean, the master scientist Sefner Quorne....

Book Four: *The Amethyst City*

The metaphysical union of the Amazon and Abna results in the mental creation of a fully mature daughter— Viona. Quorne, still struggling for domination, forces Viona into a marriage ceremony, and impregnates her. But with the intervention of Tarnec Brodix, a super-mind from an external universe, Quorne and Viona are separately flung into an ultra-dimensional limbo. Abna chooses to follow after his daughter, leaving the Amazon to brood over the disaster, alone in the Amethyst City of Saturn.

Book Five: *Daughter of the Amazon*

A miscalculation by the super-mathematician Tarnec Brodix destroys his universe, and the fault spreads into the Earth universe in the form of a Dark Tide of Absolute Nothingness. Unable to save himself, Brodix transfers his knowledge into the one mind powerful enough to receive it: that if Sefian, the son who has been born to Viona and Quorne. Sefian rapidly evolves, and, no longer human, after saving the Earth universe, vanishes into the greater universe, to seek new challenges. Then the Amazon is confronted with a further puzzle—a large section of the planet Neptune is discovered to be an exact duplicate of the Earth!

Book Six: *Quorne Returns*

The bacterial intelligences of Neptune plan to conquer Earth by replacing humans in key positions with alien duplicates. The Neptunians are themselves subjugated by the sinister Atlantean scientist, Sefner Quorne. Alerted to the threat, the Golden Amazon hits back by creating the ultimate doomsday weapon—only to precipitate a reprisal from the denizens of another universe....

Book Seven: *The Central Intelligence*

The Golden Amazon's arch-enemy, Sefner Quorne, discovers that all mental gifts, such as memory and creativity, are something that is broadcast throughout the universe by a Central Intelligence—and then interpreted according to the quality of the individual brain of the recipient. At the surprising suggestion of his wife, Viona, the Amazon's daughter, Quorne travels with her to the very center of the universe, in order to wrest the secrets of mentality from the very source itself!

Book Eight: *The Cosmic Crusaders*

The Golden Amazon renounces all ties with Earth when, together with her husband, Abna, and her daughter, Viona, she sets off on a journey to explore the cosmos. On the strange worlds of Alpha Centauri, she encounters Mizanu, the embodiment of evil—a planet-sized hypertrophied brain! Its baleful, crushing mental power threatens to reach out beyond the double-system of Alpha and Proxima Centauri to engulf the Earth and all the other inhabited planets of the galaxy—unless the Amazon can destroy it first!

Book Nine: *Parasite Planet*

The Cosmic Crusaders discover a fantastic world of mental parasites drawing form and substance from our own Earth, fifty light years distant. The planet is ruled by a being identical to the Golden Amazon herself— but an Amazon who's coldly scientific and vicious, mirroring the original Amazon as she had once been early in her career. Inevitably, they become locked in a deadly duel—to the death!

Book Ten: *World Out of Step*

The Cosmic Crusaders find themselves on a planet that seems mysteriously not to conform with natural law, a world out of step with the universe. It leaps ahead into time at unexpected moments, thereby suddenly adding many years of age to the flower-like inhabitants, and killing tens of thousands of individuals through death and old age. In trying to find the alien menace respon-sible, The Golden Amazon and her fellow Crusaders are flung backwards and forwards through time and space, threatening their own survival....

Book Eleven: *The Shadow People*

The Cosmic Crusaders discover a planet whose people are subject to a baleful influence from outer space that sweeps across their world—and for a brief while embraces every man, woman and child. It stirs the emotions of the sexes against each other. Men desire only to destroy women, and women men. Only those with higher types of mind are able to build a resistance against it. The struggle is dire and dreadful, and leaves its victims physical and mental wrecks. The less fortunate are left dead after the Wave has passed.

But when the Crusaders identify and destroy the source of the problem, they precipitate an even greater menace....

Book Twelve: *Kingpin Planet*

The Cosmic Crusaders are plunged into a strange new space, where all the probabilities of electronic law were strangely altered, a complete and stunning inversion of the so-called natural laws. They discover the mysterious silver planet of Tuca, and deep below its surface they find an enigmatic machine—the legacy of a vanished race. Masters of science, they had overreached themselves by constructing a strange machine that could alter the very laws of nature and electronic probability. The machine had ultimately destroyed them, and blasted a neighboring planet into a cosmic cinder—and unless the Cosmic Crusaders can stop it, it may well destroy the entire universe!

CHAPTER ONE
THE PROBABILITY MACHINE

With the gentleness of a bird alighting on a branch, the multi-ton mass of the spaceship *Ultra* came to rest upon a barren world—one world in countless thousands strewn throughout the complex star system of the Milky Way Galaxy. A world so far from Earth, the distance would be beyond imagination.

The throb of the massive atomic power plant whined down into silence, and with a matter-of-fact gesture Abna of Jupiter pulled out the master-switch, and then surveyed.

To land on another world was no novelty for the four who congregated around the vast observation window. Traveling through the deeps of space, their avowed intention was to bring scientific knowledge and uplift to those people of other worlds who might need it. To this end, the Cosmic Crusaders were prepared to devote their knowledge, wealth, and superhuman strength… and what was more, they were well capable of it.

Abna, the seven-foot, godlike, one-time ruler of Jupiter, was technically the leader of the quartet, but in every branch of science, save perhaps pure metaphysics, he was equaled by his phenomenally beautiful blonde wife, the Golden Amazon of Earth, eternally youthful and stupendously strong. The lesser lights in the circle of four were Viona, daughter of Abna and the Amazon, and Mexone, her husband, originally an inhabitant of a far-off world.

So, then, these four gazed upon the rocks and clouds of the deserted world to which they had come, and presently they glanced at each other.

"Nice little bit of untenanted rock," Abna said. "I think it will suit admirably."

The Amazon shrugged. "Up to you. You said you wanted somewhere quiet to work, and I can't imagine anything quieter than this. We've circumnavigated the planet and there isn't a thing on it, except rock."

Viona turned from surveying, the amber sunlight setting off the glory of her coppery hair.

"I'm still not entirely clear what we're here for," she said. "Did you say something about a machine, Dad? We've been cruising around for such a long time I've almost forgotten."

Abna indicated a series of photographs lying on the control panel bench.

"I propose to reconstruct the Probability Machine which gave us such a lot of trouble on the planet Tuca. You remember that at one stage I was projected by its probability waves into another space altogether—and there I glimpsed a world whereon natural laws don't work. In other words—putting it baldly—love becomes hate, up becomes down, and backwards becomes forward. A complete inversion of natural laws."

"And being of an inquisitive turn of mind, you want to find out more about it?" the Amazon asked dryly. "Well, I'm quite willing, even though I can't believe that the sort of planet you mention is scientifically possible."

"It isn't," Abna said simply. "Yet there it was. Now, having made that clear, let's get busy."

The Probability Machine to which he referred was complicated beyond belief, and had been dismantled stage by stage on the planet Tuca from sheer necessity. The machine, a product of trained scientists, incorporated waves of spatial stress, which, in turn, influenced the probability laws governing all matter. Working on the basis that atoms and their attendant electrons exist only in probability—a law long ago laid down by the Earthly German scientist Heisenberg—the machine was capable of disturbing the spatial probabilities to an amazing extent, even to shifting matter itself to an entirely new space—as had happened in the case of Abna when he had found himself unexpectedly projected.

Such a machine was of profound interest to the Crusaders, and in the knowledge that one day they would have a chance to study its workings in peace, Abna had photographed every intricate detail—photography of the nth degree, done to scale, stereoscopic, and in color. These prints, together with memory, would he more than sufficient to build the machine again in happier circumstances than before.

Accordingly, the four set to work, each one so versed in the arts of science that they did not need to ask questions. Abna divided the four photographic prints among the four of them, and the amazing machine tools incorporated in the *Ultra*'s equipment did the rest. Hour by hour there began to appear in the *Ultra*'s enormous workshop in the rear of the ship a tall, complicated electronic apparatus.

The four did not hurry themselves: there was no urgency about the business, and they had all the time they needed. In between spells of work and intensive concentration, they relaxed for eating or sleeping, or to log details of the barren planet to which they had come. At other times they look advantage of the planet's brief night to survey the wonder of this front-seat view of the Milky Way with its vast iridescence of stardust. Tens of thousands of worlds and suns. Unimaginable populations—and beyond the Milky Way again that other strange ultra-space, which Abna had seen. It was small wonder that the Crusaders, constantly viewing such marvels, had minds that were almost godlike.

In all, it took a fortnight to complete the Probability Machine. It was powered atomically in a self-contained unit, and therefore, unlike its prototype, it was portable, even though there was no intention as yet to move the machine from where it stood in the workshop.

"As I reason it," Abna said thoughtfully, as he and the others surveyed the completed apparatus, "this instrument works in five stages—the fifth stage being the ultimate one, and the one which projected me into that other space. It's plain from what we've learned that it did it by transposing my electronic makeup into another field of probability altogether, a field arrived at by mathematical computation within the machine itself. Even yet its profounder mathematical workings are beyond us. We know what it does, but we don't know how."

"Which is often the case with scientific things, Mexone observed. "A catalyst, for instance."

Abna nodded. "Quite so. Therefore we shall have to use Stage Five, as we'll call it, and trust to luck that it repeats the effect."

"You don't intend to project yourself with no more to go on that that, surely?" the Amazon protested; and with a smile Abna shook his head.

"No. Last time the power was beyond control. This lime we have a time unit fixed which will make for a reversal of the process when we require it. I propose to send a preset movie camera that will begin to operate when Stage Five has reached maximum power. And I'm going to do it right now."

The others watched as he placed the already adjusted movie camera in position, directly in line with the machine's main power outlet—which resembled a fantastic snout of lenses. Only the lenses were not glass: they were of a transparent substance specially devised to allow free passage of radiation.

"Here we go," Abna murmured, and depressed the power switch.

Instantly there was a deep humming from the

machine, and a vivid display of internal pyrotechnics, visible through the transparent inspection window— then things began to happen. The cine-camera became hazed with an irregular ball of orange-colored light. It did not last long. It expanded rapidly, the camera becoming transparent as it did so. Finally there was a brief tremoring of the air from underlying shock waves, and with that the orange glow vanished, and the camera, too.

Abna turned and grinned. "One perfectly good camera should now be in ultra-space," he said. "Photographing whatever happens to be in the field of view. It'll come back automatically in ten minutes."

He was right. When the time had elapsed, there was a sudden reappearance of the orange haze and in it there appeared the camera, gradually taking on density. Abna waited until the process was complete and then he switched off. Going over to the camera, he picked it up and examined it eagerly. It was unharmed—not even scratched—and had made its ten-minute recording.

"Everything all right?" the Amazon asked.

"Perfect." Abna connected the camera to a viewing screen, and then switched off the lights. In silence they sat watching the cine-recording, each busy with specu- lations.

The ultra-space transition evidently commenced in the void itself—or at any rate that was where the cine- camera had started to pick things up. There was a view of completely unfamiliar stars, certainly not belonging to the Milky Way, and a vision of a planet comparatively near. Wrapped in cloud, it gave no clue as to what lay on its surface.

"Doesn't tell us much," the Amazon said, sitting back in her chair and musing. "Looks the same as any other world to me, even if it is in another space. What gave you the idea that things went backwards?"

"I sensed it," Abna said, switching off. "Can't you understand that at that time—brief though it was—I was almost exalted? I knew of the strangeness of the planet, and was convinced of it. I'll swear it was not an illusion. I glimpsed people, too."

There was silence for a moment, then Mexone made a comment.

"Just as well that camera didn't actually hit the planet. It would have been either burned up or smashed to bits, at that speed. The time ran out at just the right moment."

Abna nodded, then looked seriously at the faces turned toward him,

"We haven't learned much, beyond the fact that I was right," he said. "Do we have a look at this world, or not?"

"Naturally!" the Amazon said promptly. "Any planet that has a puzzle attached to it is right for us. You two think the same?"

Viona and Mexone nodded promptly. Though they did not say so, they were becoming increasingly bored with the sameness of everything.

"Very well then," Abna said. "Let's make our arrangements and get started. We'll have to adjust the

Probability Machine so that its influence incorporates the whole vessel. That way we ought to get projected into this other space."

The Amazon, Viona, and Mexone took their places on the wall couches and made themselves ready for the takeoff.

"Ready?" Abna inquired, and at the murmurs of assent he engaged the ship's drive. Instantly the *Ultra*'s huge mass rose swiftly from the desolate plain and swept upwards to the murky clouds. In seconds of time the clouds were left behind and there appeared the infinite darkness of space with its endless parade of gleaming stars.

CHAPTER TWO
BACKWARDS LIFE

Motionless, Abna kept his attention on the chronometer, marking the disappearing seconds of the five minutes he had fixed. As the fourth minute was reached, he glanced at the three in their pressure beds.

"I don't know exactly what will happen when the Probability Machine operates," he said, "but from my own experience I'll guarantee that it won't be pleasant—so steel yourselves."

Fifteen seconds later the Probability Machine took over, and the four were instantly aware of the fact.... It was a distressing, anguishing experience, this turning aside into a new space, yet in many ways it was identical to the sensation the four had experienced many times in the past—a twisting and turning of body, nerve, and mentality, a sense of enormous extension and strain as atoms and molecules were torn out of their normal tracks and reformed.... Then, at last, a dead calm.

Slowly the Amazon got control of herself again, levered herself out of the pressure couch, and crossed over to where Abna was gazing through the observation window. He was breathing heavily as the result of his experiences.

"That's the planet—over there," he said.

Then Viona and Mexone came over to the window and joined Abna and the Amazon in gazing outside. The mystery world with its clouds of vapors was perhaps fifteen million miles away, as large as a rather small moon seen from Earth.

"Have you noticed, Dad, that that planet isn't an isolated one?" Viona asked. "It's one of six planets—a complete system. And that blue-white star for a sun."

"I had no time to notice things like that," Abna responded. "It doesn't particularly matter now. I do know that planet is our main objective."

So, presently, moving at high velocity, they reached the outer edge of the planet's atmosphere. Abna leveled the *Ultra* out so as to be parallel with the cloud belts, and thus began a swift circumnavigation of the globe, slackening speed and dropping lower all the time... until finally the *Ultra* was beneath the cloud banks and skimming over a flat plain, mainly composed of sand with outcroppings of vegetation and rock here and there.

"Not very impressive," the Amazon commented, staring below. "The sort of thing one might see if one happened to glimpse the Sahara on first visiting Earth."

"There's something over there, on the edge of the desert," Viona said quickly, gazing into distance. "I may be crazy, but it looks to me like a town."

"We can do two things," Abna said. "One is land in this jungle and go back on foot to the town: the other is to take a chance, circle around, and go back to the town in the *Ultra*. But it won't be easy to find a landing ground large enough…. Take your choice."

"I suggest we land in the jungle," the Amazon said. "It's easier to approach a strange race when we haven't the *Ultra* with us. Its size seems to overawe them."

"Besides," Viona added, "we want to see what sort of vegetation this planet's got."

The issue decided, Abna concentrated his attention on bringing the vessel to rest—a none-too-easy task with no sign of a clearing. Also, he was fast losing height. Finally he had to take a chance, and the result was that the multi-ton mass crashed through the topmost branches of the trees, tore down vegetation and creepers in its path, and finally alighted with considerable force in the carpeting undergrowth.

Lying somewhat upended, with a trail of destruction pointing back to the sky, the *Ultra* became still, and the throb of its power plant abruptly ceased. Abna turned from the control board and grinned.

"Sorry," he apologized. "Only thing I could do. Luckily for us, the *Ultra* is a darned sight tougher than the trees."

The Amazon opened her mouth to speak, but no words came. Instead she looked through the rear observation window in amazement. Forgetful of everything else, she hurried to it and gazed outside.

"By all that's extraordinary!" she exclaimed finally, and somewhat puzzled, the others came to her side.

"What is?" Abna asked curiously.

"Look!" She pointed in the direction they had come. "We smashed trees and branches down as we tore through them: I distinctly remember that. Yet now there isn't anything to show where we came!"

They stood in silence for a moment or two, trying to weigh up the unusual situation; then Abna, who had been gazing absently outside at some of the lower growths, suddenly gave a start. He went closer to the window and peered intently.

"Either I'm crazy," he said finally, "or these bushes outside here—the low-down ones—are growing back-wards!"

The leaves were visibly curling up slowly into sticky projections, and then decreasing into obvious buds. The actual stems of the bushes, too, were gradually shrinking in length and seemingly withdrawing into the main stem.

"Now do you believe me?" Abna asked the Amazon dryly. "I know it's against all scientific or any other law, but it's happening. Backwards life!"

"I believe it because I see it," the Amazon answered. "But I certainly want to know more about it. Let's see what the external conditions are like."

She examined instruments giving readings on the exterior conditions, and made a quick analysis of the air sample, which she extracted in an ampule. The results were satisfactory.

"Oxygen, hydrogen, krypton, and nitrogen," she announced. "In quantities quite suitable for our type of life. Temperature around seventy degrees Fahrenheit, so that's no hardship."

"Before long," Abna said, operating the control that opened the airlock, "I fancy that somebody will come looking for us. We must have been seen as we crossed that town—and since the *Ultra* is not the kind of object seen every day, I imagine we'll have a visitation. We'd better be well armed and ready."

The Amazon inspected the instrument and weapon belt about her waist and then relaxed again, satisfied. Abna, Viona and Mexone checked their own weapons, and then they were ready.... Once outside in the mild, soft atmosphere Abna switched over the concealed locking switch that closed the airlock and made the ship impregnable from the outside. Then he led the way to the nearest bushes.

They exhibited the same peculiarity as that seen from the window. They were definitely growing backwards. Another unusual thing was that there was nothing dead anywhere. No broken and decayed branches, no sear and yellow grass—not even a smashed blade of it at the edges of the *Ultra*'s enormous weight. Everywhere a newness, a fresh greenness—and a fantastic vision of branches everywhere shrinking with the slowness of a thread of mercury exposed to gradual cold.

There was something else, too, decidedly less positive, which the four could all feel. It was a sensation of growing irritation—even anger—out of all proportion to the circumstances. None of them had anything to be angry about, even less to be angry with each other, and yet they were. Each and every one of them.

Suddenly Abna halted. With a raised hand he made the others halt, too. They looked at him, unreasonable resentment smoldering in their eyes.

"Well, what now?" the Amazon demanded. "What have we stopped for?"

"To get ourselves straight," Abna said, plainly having something of a struggle to master himself. "If the plants can grow backwards, then it is logical to assume that love—or at any rate, affection—can take the inverse form of hatred and irritation."

The others were silent, grasping at the truth of the statement.

"You're right," the Amazon said, keeping a hold on herself. "Even so, it is going to be almost impossible to keep a constant grip on the emotions. We'll have to think of another way of exploring."

"The trouble didn't affect us inside the ship," Viona commented. "If that's any guide to what is happening."

"I believe it is," Abna said, thinking. "The *Ultra* is always shielded by a repulsive shell, electrical in basis, which stops any dangerous radiations from penetrating. So this emotional disturbance is produced by electrical means. Something must be affecting our brains."

"In that case we want insulated helmets," the Amazon said. "Hadn't we better return to the *Ultra* and manufacture some?"

Abna answered by striding back along the path they had come. Fortunately, they had traveled no great distance, otherwise the emotional repercussions might have been considerable. And once within the giant vessel they could sense the unbearable irritation relaxing as the mysterious influence, whatever it was, was cut off.

The manufacture of the protective helmets, which fitted in the fashion of skullcaps, was a simple job with the workshop's infinite resources—then, thus protected, they set off again through the jungle, and no hint of emotional disturbance touched them.

Then suddenly the people of this fantastic world became visible—six of them, dressed in one-piece, lilac-colored tunics. They were human enough in appearance, though rather below average size. The curious thing about them was that they kept their distance from each other. Each one was separated from his neighbor by about six feet. Apparently they were not particularly hostile, for they carried no weapons.

Emerging completely from the forest, they stood staring with round, big-pupiled eyes, an expression of infinite puzzlement on their faces.

"Look harmless enough," the Amazon murmured, taking her hand away from her proton gun. "See what you can do with them, Abna."

Abna raised a powerful hand. "Friends," he said deliberately. "We come as friends."

The reply from one of them sounded a mere gabble of words, but in a questioning tone. Abna shook his head and sighed.

"Language trouble," he said, glancing at the Amazon. "We will only get over it by taking them to the *Ultra* and giving them a session with the Language

Instructor."

"If they'll come," the Amazon answered doubtfully.

It was worth a try, anyhow. By signs Abna showed what he wanted, pointing back along the trail, and after a moment the men of this queer planet seemed to comprehend. Quite willingly, but still maintaining their distance from each other, they began to follow as Abna led the way. And they continued to follow through the whole distance, pausing at last to look in silent awe upon the immense mass of the *Ultra*. Even then they did not converse with each other, maintaining their odd separation.

Abna opened the airlock and led the way into the control room, after which he had some trouble in making the six men understand that they were not in any way in danger. Finally one of them seemed willing to take a chance, and cautiously entered the control room to look about him.

From this beginning Abna went by easy stages, until he had completely secured the man's confidence— then, with the other men peering in interestedly at the doorway, he went to work with the Language Instructor, a helmet controlled electrically which, when placed on the head, automatically transferred all the knowledge required concerning the English language, as well as the identities of the four Crusaders.

In a matter of ten minutes the transference of knowledge was complete. Abna removed the helmet and smiled down on the little man as he rubbed his forehead in puzzled wonder.

"Everything all right, my friend?" he inquired, smiling.

"Yes. Yes, everything's all right, even though I do not understand how I am able to speak your language. You are a worker of great scientific marvels."

"Do you wish me to transfer language to your comrades, so they may understand what is transpiring?"

"That is unnecessary, Abna. I can tell them what you have to tell me. I am the leader. And none of us gives to the other any more than he can help."

Abna glanced at the Amazon. Both of them were vaguely puzzled by this remarkably selfish outlook.

"From where do you come, Abna?" the little man asked. "We saw your machine cross our town and knew it had fallen somewhere, so we came to look for it. My name is Disi, of the planet Umnol."

"Greetings," Abna replied gravely. "We come from a world so far away its distance would be meaningless to you. We are indeed from another space entirely, beyond this one—or perhaps that doesn't make sense to you?"

"It makes perfect sense," Disi responded surprisingly. "We have a fair knowledge of science, though not of space travel. Indeed, we hope by science to save ourselves from disaster."

"Oh?" Immediately Abna was on the alert.

"It is a long story," the little man said, "but still one which you may care to hear. The wonder of a visit from beings of another world rouses me to a realization of my duties. Would you care to be my guests?"

Abna, though he smiled at the man's grandiloquent use of his new-found language, nodded politely.

"We would be delighted to accompany you, Disi. There is a lot we wish to learn about you—and on the other hand, there is probably much that you wish to know about us."

CHAPTER THREE
DEEPENING MYSTERY

In about an hour, following a journey through a forest that had become sparser and smaller, Disi's town was reached—the same one that the four had seen from the *Ultra* as they had flown over it. As towns go, it was quite a normal one and covered a goodish area, entrance to it being gained by a long, straight roadway which went straight as an arrow to the heart of the buildings and intersecting roadways. A vehicle, on the style of an automobile, was parked at the end of the street where jungle and street interwove, and toward this Disi marched with solemn dignity with his five colleagues spaced out at the usual discreet distance behind.

Whatever preconceived notions the quartet might have had about the efficiency of the vehicle they entered, they were soon dispelled when they experienced its terrific rocket-like speed. In a matter of seconds it had shot down the length of the main street, apparently missing other similar vehicles by inches, finally pulling up in the wide grounds around one detached building in particular.

"If you will come this way," Disi murmured, quite unconcerned as he opened the vehicle's door. "This is the building from which control of the city is operated. In other words, my own domain."

He alighted from the vehicle and led the way across the grounds, up the building steps, and eventually into a broad, lounge-like room with big windows. The room was comfortably furnished with earthly-looking appointments, so much so that it was hard to realize this was a strange world in another space.

Abna, the Amazon, Viona, and Mexone all sat down on a huge couch-like affair, and waited for the next move. The colleagues of Disi were briefly dismissed, and the door closed.

"You would care for refreshment?" Disi inquired, and as Abna nodded assent the little man lifted an object like a speaking tube, gave a few brief instructions through it in his own language, and then he settled on a nearby chair. In silence the four looked at him, weighing him up. It was odd, but although he evidently had a good deal of authority, he looked surprisingly young—not more than perhaps twenty.

"Your hospitality is much appreciated, Disi," Abna commented, breaking the silence. "Naturally, we do not wish to take up too much of your time, for you must obviously be a busy man."

"Busy—yes, but with only one objective. Trying to stave off inevitable disaster."

"You've mentioned that before," the Amazon reminded him. "What disaster?"

Disi smiled a trifle wanly. "It would not interest you my friends. In fact, you would probably not even understand it. I do not wish to burden you with my troubles. Let us exchange information, and scientific news if possible, and there finish."

Abna was about to reply when two servants appeared with loaded trays of food. He looked at them curiously. They were girls of not more than twelve years of age, elfinly pretty and extremely quiet. Without a word they set the trays down then, keeping a good distance from each other, they made their departure.

"Help yourselves, my friends," Disi invited motioning to the trays. "I trust our type of food will not be injurious to you."

A few experimental mouthfuls by Abna and the Amazon settled the issue—as far as Viona and Mexone were concerned. The food of Umnol was pure enough, though mainly fruit-like. Whatever its nature, it had a pleasant taste and was surprisingly stimulating.

"Only a little while ago," Disi said, "those two young girls whom you have just seen were middle-aged women. And I, at the same time, was of considerable maturity. That might help to explain the nature of the thing we are fighting."

"In other words," the Amazon said slowly, "they have grown younger, even as you have?"

"Exactly. Not only have they grown younger, but their stature has decreased in conformity with their youth. In the end they will return to babyhood, then to the embryo, and finally will disappear altogether."

For a while the four ate in silence, thinking busily nonetheless. Then Abna asked a question.

"Has this extraordinary condition always been present on this planet?"

"As far as we know, yes." Disi mused for a moment. "Were it not for that, we could have a go-ahead, pleasant world here. We do a good deal of trading among ourselves, have a fair science, and are generally happy—but the planet is so utterly mysterious, and its laws so queer, that we never feel safe."

"How are you born?" asked Viona thoughtfully, and Disi glanced at her.

"We are not born," he said simply. "We simply come into being at an age of extreme maturity—what one would call the advanced prime of life—and from that moment we start to grow younger, men and women alike. And we have no memory of how we came into being. We just do."

"And emotions?" the Amazon asked curiously. "Have you any at all?"

Disi sighed. "As I have said, what emotions we have, which any thinking creature must possess, are all in reverse to what we want. We love somebody intensely, only to find that against our will it becomes hate. We may be joyful about something, but rapidly it sours and becomes sorrow."

"There is no marriage?" Abna questioned.

"Marriage is unknown. The love that begets marriage is here only interpreted as hatred—so, of course, it is an impossible state. There are no genuine children, either—only those who have grown backwards from maturity to child life. And the babies are the ones to be pitied, for soon they will cease to exist, and having no parents, they become the responsibility of the state."

"For all this," Abna said, his food forgotten, "there has most certainly got to be an answer, my friend—and perhaps we can help you find it. Already we have mastered the trouble of reversed emotions, so perhaps we can solve the rest."

Disi turned from the window in surprise "But why should you wish to? It is really no problem of yours."

"In a way it is," Abna replied, half smiling. "For one thing we have science which is far and away ahead of yours in the matter of efficiency, and we have also immense experience in cosmic problems. For that very reason we call ourselves the Cosmic Crusaders. We're dedicated to the job of trying to help unfortunate races out of difficulties."

Disi came back slowly from the window. "But where would you start to solve this mystery? We have tried in every way we know to get to the bottom of it, and have never succeeded."

Abna said: "Give us complete freedom of movement to study the situation, and I don't doubt but what we'll be able to arrive at some solution."

It was clear from his manner that Disi did not think for a moment that anything could be done—nevertheless he was willing to take a gamble.

"You are my guests for as long as you wish," he said. "I will see to it that rooms are prepared for you here in my government building, and you shall be free to come and go as you please. But I warn you, expect difficulties."

"We're used to them," Abna smiled, continuing with his meal. "Do you mean difficulties from people, or from conditions?"

"Conditions. To a certain extent we live in the forward sense—in the matter of eating, sleeping, and so forth, but every now and again we realize with horrible clearness how much our surroundings are going backwards all the time. It may happen to you. Something you are relying upon will suddenly not be there, devolved to a state before it existed, and therefore ceasing to be. I warn you: this is a paradox of a planet; how much so you'll only find out as you become acquainted more fully with it."

"Our main base of operations will be the *Ultra*," Abna said. "That's our spaceship. We have the necessary equipment there to perform whatever tests and experiments we need. Apart from that, we will be glad to accept your hospitality." He glanced toward the window. "How much time have we before night comes?"

"About four hours. You have noticed perhaps that this world of Umnol rotates in the opposite direction to the other planets in the system?"

"We've noticed," the Amazon said, musing.

"This will sound odd to you, but tomorrow is really yesterday because the planet is moving from future to past all the time. That doesn't mean that all the things that happen on it are yesterday's occurrences, but it docs mean that with every revolution the planet grows younger. Like a clock that is going backwards, and thus showing a constant retrogression of time."

The four looked at each other, only just beginning to realize how really complicated was the situation into which they had come.

CHAPTER FOUR
THE VANISHING NOTES

Immediately the four had finished their meal, they took their leave of Disi—with the promise to return shortly—and went back to the *Ultra*, being carried part of the way in one of the strange, immensely fast vehicles. When presently they were seated in the *Ultra*'s control room, amid familiar surroundings, they debated the matter of the backwardly condemned planet with scientific deliberation.

"Doesn't it occur to you," the Amazon said, "that these fantastic conditions may be the result of the probability wave which spread out from Tuca into this other space—the one in which you were caught up, Abna?"

"Even allowing for a different time-ratio in this region, I don't think that's the answer," Abna responded. "This weird state of affairs has been going on for ages and isn't just a recent innovation. No, we want a different answer."

"How do we start looking for it?" Viona questioned.

"I think it would be a waste of time trying," Abna shrugged. "We would do better to start working on the known conditions, and somehow neutralize them. That will save a lot of trouble for us, and the race of Umnol."

Abna rose and crossed to the instrument panel. First he switched off the shell of repulsive energy with which the *Ultra* was usually shielded—thereby leaving it open to receive whatever radiations were around it—und then he set an electrical detector in action. Silently he watched it, the others content with gazing from where they sat. Almost immediately the needle swung the full length of the graded scale, a sure indication of tremendous electrical, or at any rate spatial, disturbance. Nor did the needle move in the slightest to show any diminution.

"Well, there it is," Abna said presently. "Exactly what it is, is another matter. Maybe we'd better find out."

The Amazon got to her feet and helped him with the technical details. They consisted of carefully adjusting a compass-like device until its needle was pointing directly into the heart of the strange inflowing waves. Then by a process of calculation, and reference to the numbers on the needle dial, it was possible to deduce the wavelength and power of the waves under detection.

But this time the instrument could not grapple fully with the problem. The readings seemed to change constantly.

"What do you make of it?" Abna asked after a while.

"Only one thing," the Amazon answered slowly "I think we are working on something similar to the device we've already got—meaning the Probability

Machine. Here we are not getting normal readings. We seem unable to pin down the exact wavelength. That could happen if we were dealing with electronic probabilities instead of spatial facts. In other words, the incoming waves are postulations, and nothing more—therefore, they cannot be analyzed."

"I think you're right," Abna agreed, after a moment or two. "In which case there is only one answer. We must work out a solution on the central computer, and use our own Probability Machine to pose the question."

"How are you going to do that?" Mexone asked, puzzled.

"Reproduce on the Probability Machine a wavelength—if you can call it that—identical to this one, which obviously has something to do with Time. We'll turn the wavelength directly on to the computer and leave it to work out the details—both of the wave itself, and how to neutralize it."

"Seems the only way," the Amazon admitted; then she looked a trifle dubious, "I only hope we're not tackling things too deep for us. If somehow we repatterned Time about us, we'd be in a pretty mess."

"Have to risk it," Abna shrugged. "Give me a hand to connect the computer with the Probability Machine in the workshop."

This accomplished, Abna went back and took the readings of the compass trained on the wave. After that it was simply a matter of setting the Probability Machine's mechanism to the approximately same readings, and waiting to see what happened.

"All this points to highly intelligent minds behind the reversal business," the Amazon commented. "Minds as good as those who built the Prohability Machine on Tuca."

"Looks like it," Abna agreed, then he stepped back and motioned the others to do likewise. The Probability Machine was in operation, working on a delayed-action switch. Abna watched it intently, allowing only a few minutes for it to be in action, then he reached to the long-distance control and switched it off.

"The rest's up to the computer," he commented, as the instrument hummed busily. "And in spite of your fears, nothing seems to have happened."

The Amazon glanced about her, then nodded. Everything was normal and undisturbed.

"And when we have the answer," she said, "I suppose we devise something to produce a neutralization?"

"That's the general idea," Abna agreed. "Once we've done that, we'll look around and see if we can't find who's responsible for all this. Obviously they are doing their utmost to make life unpleasant on Umnol, but what the reason can be I can't imagine."

For a time they looked at the computer, but it was not ready yet to deliver itself of an answer. It was tackling a deeply scientific problem, one that strained its marvelous electronic interior to the utmost. In fact, darkness had come outside the *Ultra*, and Abna had replaced the repulsive shield for safety's sake before the computer at last arrived at its conclusion and printed out a sheet of paper covered with mathematical symbols.

Frowning, Abna studied the complicated formula, and the Amazon, looking with him, gave a whistle.

"This thing is divided into two parts, without any apparent indication where the dividing line comes."

"That's what I think," the Amazon agreed. "It doesn't make sense otherwise. One half is the formula of the wave which the Probability Machine projected, and the other half is a formula of neutralization."

"Exactly," Abna assented. "We'd be about 100 years trying to knock sense into the actual formula, so let's concentrate on how to neutralize—commencing with equation ninety-six."

Viona and Mexone glanced at one another and made no attempt to struggle any more. Since the Amazon and Abna had got a grasp of the situation, there was nothing more to be said: they would work it out in their own way.

And work it out they did, after three hours of solid effort. When, in the finish, their individual conclusions agreed, Abna sat back in his chair.

"For this we'll need a completely new machine," he said. "Something like the Probability Machine, but working in a reverse manner—a machine able to cancel out the probabilities that are being projected at this planet and taking form as time in reverse. With the machine tools we've got, we can do it, but it will take some time. Do you want to design the machine now, or take a rest first?"

"Rest!" the Amazon exclaimed in contempt. "With a

thing like this to gnaw at? Not likely! Let's get busy.… Viona, Mexone, get some food and restorative for us, will you?"

The younger ones nodded and went to work. Abna paused only long enough to eat and drink, then they began the designing of the machine which, on paper, would release the world of Umnol from the fantastic grip which was upon it. Blind, deaf, and dumb to everything except the designing, they worked on through the night under the bright light, while Viona and Mexone retired for rest.

It was just paling dawn in the Umnol sky when Abna relaxed and gave a yawn.

"That's it," he said. "Nothing left but to build it—and that we'll do immediately we've had a sleep. Okay?"

"Okay," the Amazon agreed.

Viona and Mexone were aroused to take over guard duty—in case anything unforeseen occurred—and then the Amazon and Abna retired to recover their energies. It was full Umnol daylight when they awoke again, to find that Viona at least had anticipated their awakening and prepared a breakfast for them.

"Anything happened?" the Amazon inquired, as she sat down, and for a moment Viona hesitated.

"Well—not exactly," she replied.

"Not exactly?" Abna repeated in surprise. "That sounds unusually vague for you, Viona."

She glanced across at Mexone and he seemed to interpret that as a signal for him to explain.

"There have been queer sounds, cracks and creaks

which neither of us could locate. It sounded rather like very hot metal clicking as it cools."

"Queer," the Amazon frowned. "Certainly it couldn't have been our exhaust tubes contracting, because we haven't flown anywhere. Did it go on all night?"

"Almost," Viona admitted. "You may hear it yourself before long."

Accordingly, silence was maintained and the four remained on the alert. Then presently there came a creak, to be almost instantly followed by a sharp crack, exactly like a bough breaking in the wind. Both the Amazon and Abna jerked up their heads sharply.

"I don't like it," Abna said grimly. "Something is giving way in the ship itself from the sound of things. It came from over here."

He hurried to a corner of the control room and gazed intently at the curved metal wall. At this point there was no safety padding, so his view of the metal was unimpeded. As there came another crack he started forward and looked upwards, then he gave a start of amazement.

"The metal's giving way," he exclaimed. "I can see the sky through it—faintly."

That was enough to bring the Amazon, Viona, and Mexone hurrying to his side. In consternation they found that he was right.

"What can be the reason for it?" Viona asked, dismayed.

Instead of answering immediately, Abna glanced across at the control board.

"Repulsive shield is switched on," he said. "Yes, I remember doing it after we'd had the experiment last night. There's only one explanation: we're being affected by the mysterious something which causes everything on this planet to devolve."

"With the repulsive screen on?" the Amazon protested.

"The repulsive screen isn't strong enough to resist it—that's the only explanation. I'll increase the repulsion to triple power and see how that stands up. If it doesn't, we'll try something else."

He moved across to the switch panel and made the necessary adjustments; then the Amazon glanced at him.

"They're using extraordinarily powerful waves for them to affect us like this.... Whoever 'they' may be."

"No doubt of it," Abna agreed, "and this is a way which can definitely put the *Ultra* at a discount. In a test of strength versus strength, this metal can stand anything."

They spent several anxious minutes watching the thinned metal wall, but there was no sign of it becoming worse. After about half an hour Abna relaxed a trifle.

"I think we've managed it. We'll reseal that portion with fresh metal just for safety—though probably when we've stopped this influence, it will revert to normal anyway."

"Sooner we get this influence under control and completely neutralized, the better," the Amazon said. "Better start building that neutralizer machine, hadn't we, Abna?"

He nodded. All thought of resuming their interrupted breakfast had gone now: they were interested only in putting a stop to the menace which was doing its best to catch up with them.

Abna moved to the side bench, his mind intent on studying the designs he and the Amazon had completed the previous night. Then he paused, staring incredulously. Abruptly he looked at Viona as she cleared away the remains of their meal.

"Viona, have you moved anything away from here?"

"Moved anything? Why, no. What, for instance?"

Abna did not answer. He motioned to the Amazon and she came over to him. In complete astonishment she stared down at the papers upon which they had worked so hard the previous night. The papers were blank, as too were the scratch pads that had contained all their precious computations.

Abna sighed, and at that the Amazon glanced at him.

"That time business again," he said bitterly. "During the night it must have penetrated the repulsive shield and it has eliminated all the notes we made! Hours of work thrown down the drain! Disi was right when he warned us we'd experience many odd things."

"It's going to be a terrible job doing it all again," the Amazon said.

"I'm not so sure that we're going to," Abna muttered. "We have no guarantee but what the same thing won't happen again."

"Surely not? The repulsive screen will prevent it."

"We hope it will, but we can't be sure. Anyway, I don't think it's a good risk. Apart from that, there's another consideration."

"Such as?"

"I've just been thinking. Doesn't it occur to you that even if we did neutralize this time trouble, it would only be a temporary measure?"

"Yes—maybe you're right," the Amazon admitted. "And yet what other way have we of dealing with the trouble?"

"I think," Abna said, "the best course would be to get one of these people when they first appear on the planet. We have the necessary instruments for brain-reading. From a study of a newcomer's brain it might be possible to discover their point of origin. Once we do, we'll go further."

The Amazon reflected over the plan for a moment or two and then nodded.

"Seems reasonable enough," she agreed. "We'd better have another word or two with Disi and learn a bit more about the way people appear on this world."

"And we might do worse than let him have the formula for these helmets we're wearing—or rather skullcaps," Abna went on. "If we can mass produce them for the race, they can at least be sure of their emotions behaving normally without outside interference, and it might also cause them to cease evolving into a younger state. The body can only obey the mind, and if the mind is protected, I see no reason why they should not behave naturally."

"What are we waiting for?" the Amazon asked, crossing to the switch panel and airlock control. "Viona, Mexone—you'd better come along with us."

CHAPTER FIVE
THE GOLDEN RAY

When he found the four Crusaders back once more in his domain, Disi was obviously pleased. He seemed to extract a certain amount of assurance from the knowledge that the four were present and trying to help him.

Disi listened attentively to Abna's scheme of trying to get hold of a newly materialized person, in order to read the brain. It was plain he did not know how such a thing was going to be done, but he was co-operative enough.

"It so happens that a woman appeared only this morning," he said. "Like all the others of our race she had no idea where she came from, and is at present in the state's charge to be educated into our ways. I can have her brought as a suitable person for your experiment if you wish."

"Please do so," Abna said promptly.

He waited while Disi gave the necessary instructions to one of the girl servants, then he resumed, explaining the virtues of the skullcaps, which he and the others were wearing.

"We have the metals you mention," Disi said thoughtfully, "and problems of production do not arise. I could order these skullcaps to be made in the tens of thousands—sufficient for my own immediate people, and for other towns in different parts of the planet. But do you, in all honesty, think they would prove effective?"

"Certainly I do. As I have said, the mind controls the body. With the mind effectually insulated, the body must follow suit and behave normally."

Disi smiled whimsically. "Your science is of an order which I can but feebly grasp, friend Abna. Whilst we believe the body is at the control of the brain, we believe also that the brain is sometimes affected by what happens to the body. Therefore, just insulating the brain will not do any good by our reckoning, as long as this deadly influence attacks the rest of our bodies."

"The brain is merely the organism through which the mind acts," Abna smiled. "The most sensitive part of a nervous structure. However, it can do no harm to manufacture a few of the skull-caps and see what happens."

"I will make them," Disi assented, taking the specification that Abna had written out for him. "I will translate this, then we can—"

He paused as the door opened to admit one of the girl servants. Behind her, clad in drab regulation clothes, came a woman of considerable age, white-haired and feebly-built. She looked at least eighty years of age. She stood waiting whilst the servant rattled off something in her own tongue, and then retired swiftly.

"This is the woman," Disi said. "We have given her the name of Ilviron. Like all the others, men and women, she is of considerable age, but will become gradually younger."

"Right," Abna said. "We will take charge of her and learn all we can—then we will return her safely to you. Do you wish to inform her of our intentions?"

"Needless, friend Abna. She does not as yet understand the language: she is completely unaware of anything at the moment, and will remain so until she is trained."

The four were silent, looking at the woman thoughtfully. She gazed back with lackluster blue eyes. There was complete vacancy about her expression.

"If that is all," Disi said, rising. "I will make arrangements for a vehicle to transport you to the edge of the jungle."

His orders were promptly carried out, and eventually the four found themselves back in the *Ultra*'s control room. They made a quick checkup to be sure that no further retrogression had appeared in the *Ultra*'s metalwork—which it had not—and then they turned lo the task in hand, finding in the old woman an easy and docile subject.

The woman did not protest in the least as a helmet was fitted tightly on her head, nor did she feel anything from the live electrodes fitted to its exterior—yet with every moment nearly invisible rays, so thin were they, were searching every nerve and convolution of her brain, flashing back whatever impressions they received. Later, projection would show exactly what the rays had picked up.

For nearly an hour the process was continued, until the Amazon and Abna were satisfied with their efforts. Only then was the helmet removed and the apparatus pushed on one side.

"Give her some food and drink and let her rest," Abna said. "Then join us in the projection booth while we see what we got." In five minutes Viona and Mexone had arrived, full of eagerness to see what had happened. The old woman they had bedded down comfortably on one of the pressure couches and left her with adequate food and drink, after satisfying themselves that she could feed herself.

"We certainly got something," Abna said, switching on the projector. "Now's let's see just what kind of images we've got."

The Amazon put out the lights—then attention was entirely given to the screen as recorded images were ran through. Almost immediately it gave a view of a world of verdure. There were rolling valleys and pouring sunshine, lakes and oceans, forests and hills—a world altogether lovely yet apparently unpopulated. Throughout the whole time the view was centered on this planet. At first, different parts of the planet were incorporated, and then things switched to one portion in particular—one of the valleys, remarkable for its beauty, with a gigantic cliff rearing to the cloudless sky.

Then, without any warning, an abrupt change. A

vision of the world of Umnol replaced that of the other world, and thereafter everything recorded was merely what the woman had seen and experienced since arriving on the backwardly moving planet.

"Extremely interesting," the Amazon said. "Apart from the views we got of the planet Umnol—which was plainly taken when the woman's brain was at full consciousness—I'd say that the rest of the visions were subconscious impressions which she herself will be unable to call to mind. They're memory impressions which are buried deep in the subconscious and have somehow been blotted out."

"Exactly what I think," Abna assented. "From which we can infer that the woman came originally from another world and somehow materialized here, but great care was taken by those who projected her to blot out all memory of where she had come from, as indeed apparently happens with all the men and women who appear on Umnol. How she was projected, or who was responsible for it, we don't know yet. Nor have we any idea what this strange business is all about."

"Do you suppose it could have been one of the other planets in this system?" the Amazon asked. "There are six planets in the system, don't forget, and we haven't examined any of them very thoroughly, remember."

"That we can soon remedy," Abna responded promptly. "The world which this woman's brain reveals is apparently sunny and cloudless, so if such a world is within telescopic range we'll see its surface clearly and identify it. Let's see what we can do."

Abna led the way back into the control room and then, his hand on the telescopic controls, he hesitated briefly before making up his mind.

"I think we'll take our observations from outer space where we can get a clear view. I know we've got x-ray devices on the telescope, but it'll be a long job penetrating clouds and tree vegetation."

Accordingly he switched on the plant and gave the vessel a short burst of power, which lifted it right out of the forest and through the cloudbanks into outer space. There he went into orbit, and surveyed the scene, the vapors of Umnol lying like a vast sunlit ocean below.

"…three, four, five, six," the Amazon said, indicating the other planets of the system through the observation window. "We'd better have a look at the nearest one first."

She swung the *Ultra*'s largest telescope into action, its object glass pressed flush with the warp-free purity of the observation window. Then she peered intently through the eyepieces and focused slowly. An acid-sharp view of a cloudless planet presently emerged, its surface details made up mainly of green and brown splashes.

"Looks like I hit it first time," she commented. "But more power is needed."

She swung the turret-head of eyepieces to the strongest magnification, and immediately a view of a lake and forest became visible, trembling slightly due to the atmosphere of the planet itself.

"We've got it," she murmured, moving the telescope

slowly on its smooth gimbals. "I'm looking for the cliff we saw in the film."

"Looks rather like Earth," Viona commented at length, glancing up.

"Except that the verdure is far ahead of anything Earthly," the Amazon replied. "You'll notice the profusions of flowers, too. I rather think our mystery world is a kind of paradise."

"But only to look at," Abna said grimly, with a glance toward the old woman sleeping peacefully on the pressure couch. "Unless our calculations are completely wrong, that planet is the gateway to a good deal of scientific intrigue."

There was silence for a moment, as the bountiful planet—a mere dot in the firmament when viewed without the telescope—was contemplated; then the Amazon turned to Abna.

"We go there, of course, and have a look for ourselves what is going on?"

"Definitely—but first we must return our old lady friend to Umnol. She probably wouldn't be able to stand the rigors of the journey." Abna turned from a study of the instruments. "It's approximately fifty-two million miles away. Won't take us long to get there."

So they returned to Umnol as swiftly as possible, returned the old woman to the care of Disi, and explained to him what they had learned, and what they intended doing. Then they were away, rapidly leaving the incredible Umnol behind and sweeping through the depths of this strange space with ever-mounting speed. To a ship with the almost limitless velocity of the *Ultra*, fifty-two million miles was a mere hop. Very soon the cloudless planet was looming below, its landscape becoming ever clearer as the *Ultra* began to drop.

"About the most beautiful planet we've ever yet seen," the Amazon commented, surveying. "Wonder if its atmosphere is as good as it looks."

A few moments later as they entered the atmospheric envelope she made the necessary analysis, and then nodded in rather surprised approval.

"Perfect!" she announced, as the others glanced questioningly. "A little more oxygen than we're used to, but that's all to the good. There seems to be almost an absence of water vapor, which no doubt accounts for there being no clouds."

Abna nodded and turned to the switchboard. Carefully he brought the machine down into the heart of a valley.

"Still looks inviting," Viona said, standing by the window. "And there doesn't seem to be a trace of anybody around."

"I think you're right enough there," the Amazon replied. "There hasn't been a sign of life all the time we've had the planet under observation. Better get outside, hadn't we, and have a look around?" She cut off the repulsive screen, and turned.

A check was made of weapons, just in case. Then Abna depressed the switch that opened the airlock. When the door had swung wide he stood looking outside, sniffing gently at the air.

"Beautiful!" he exclaimed in rapture. "Absolutely beautiful! Smells just like a perfume factory."

The others as they followed him out into the blazing sunshine, soon discovered what he meant. The air smelled of lavender, neither too little or too much— just enough to give a delicious fragrance. The beautiful aroma, together with the hot sunshine and the warm breeze, coupled with the curiously soft ground and brilliant green vegetation, gave a Garden of Eden quality to the surroundings.

"Where exactly are we going?" the Amazon asked, after they had been walking for a while.

"Nowhere in particular," Abna answered her, glancing back at the giant mass of the *Ultra*. "We're simply walking for the pleasure of it as far as I'm concerned.... Just the same," he broke off, stifling a yawn, "I am beginning to feel oddly sleepy."

They walked for a while in the soft ground, glancing about them interestedly, then suddenly Abna came to a stop and looked at his feet. The Amazon glanced in surprise.

"Anything wrong?" she asked.

"I'm not quite sure. I was just thinking it remarkable that this stuff we're walking on isn't soil, rock, or anything else I ever saw. Looks like powdered chemical of some kind."

Surprised by the statement, the Amazon stopped to look, then scooped up a handful and examined it carefully. As Abna had said, it was not ordinary soil but seemed to be a mixture of various elements.

"From the look of things," Abna went on, "the whole surface of the planet is made up of stuff like this. You'd better keep that lot you've collected for analysis."

The Amazon promptly put the stuff in the small specimen bag she carried on her waist-belt, and then the walking continued—but not for very long. Viona was the first to show that the creeping tiredness that was making itself felt was a very real thing.

"This may seem crazy," she said yawning widely, "but I'm too tired to go any farther. I'm absolutely dead-beat. Let's rest for a while."

She did not wait to see if the others agreed. She flopped down just where she was and sprawled luxuriously in strange soil. Her eyes began to close even as she lay.

"Might as well follow her example," Abna suggested. "I admit I never felt so exhausted before."

"No! Wait a minute!" the Amazon snapped, forcing herself to remain alert. "If we once start to sleep we may never wake up. Hasn't it occurred to you that we may be drugged?"

Abna started. "Drugged! By what?"

"This lavender perfume perhaps.... It's everywhere, and somehow it deadens the senses—" The Amazon stopped and looked at Viona as she sprawled in the luxury of sleep. But only for a moment then the Amazon's hand shot down and hauled her, protesting, to her feet.

"Oh, what's the idea?" Viona grumbled, still only

half awake. "I'm tired, I tell you! Leave me be!"

"Wake up!" the Amazon snapped. "For your own good!"

Viona reeled a little in her mother's grasp, fast fading off into sleep, until a stinging blow across her face temporarily aroused her again.

"Sorry," the Amazon apologized. "That was for your own sake! Let's get back to the ship while we're still conscious."

Which was not half so easy a job as it seemed. With every step they took from now they felt weighted down by a force of countless tons. They literally dragged their limbs, and ever and again they faded into sleep as they walked, only to be violently slapped and jerked back to life by one or the other. In this wise they managed the journey and finally crawled into the control room. Abna had just enough strength left to snap the airlock switch, then he dropped full length into dreamless slumber.

He was the first to awaken again, and as near as he could judge from the chronometer, he had been unconscious for three hours. Even now he felt groggy, with a dryness in his mouth and a smell of lavender in his nostrils—but it was a condition that did not last long. With the return of his faculties and particularly the use of his mind, he rapidly mastered the remainder and then set to work to revive the others.

Finally, as they sat sipping restoratives, they looked at each other questioningly.

"Good job you had the wit to realize what was

happening," Abna said, looking at the Amazon. "We'd have been out cold for good otherwise. With normal air in here, we slowly recovered."

"Well, what do we do now?" Mexone asked, gazing through the window. "Now we've arrived in the Garden of Eden it seems as though we can't do anything about it. And we certainly haven't learned anything worth while."

"We could, of course, go out in space suits and try to learn something that way," the Amazon said, "but after what's happened I think our best bet would be to stay inside the *Ultra* and explore the planet. There must have been some reason for that old woman having seen this planet before she appeared on Umnol—"

The Amazon paused and looked down at herself. Quite unconsciously she had latched her thumbs in her belt, and that had brought her right hand in contact with the small specimen bag. She unhooked it and looked at it carefully.

"I'd forgotten all about this. Let's see what sort of a soil they've got on this planet."

The analysis, with Abna helping, did not take long—but when it was over, both the Amazon and Abna were frowning.

"Anything peculiar?" Viona asked, coming over to them.

"Not exactly," Abna told her, "but certainly something quite unique. This stuff isn't soil at all—it's made up of a variety of elements. We have sulphur, a form of sugar, phosphorus, slight traces of magnesium, some salt, iron, and quite a few fatty substances. Last of all we have liquid water, with a strong ammonia content—which accounts for the ground being so curiously resilient and spongy. Add to that a trace of fatty acids, and that's the makeup."

"Interesting, but not very informative," was Viona's comment.

As Viona wandered away to join Mexone in gazing through the observation window the Amazon said slowly: "I know this formula, Abna, but I can't exactly place it. It is the formula for something quite common, though whether these ingredients are here by accident or design is another matter. Perhaps we—"

"Hey!" Viona shouted abruptly. "Come and look here!"

Immediately, impressed by her earnestness, the Amazon and Abna hurried to her side. They gave a start as they beheld the sight that was fascinating her—a shaft of golden-yellow light, certainly not from the sun, projecting downwards from the blue sky. Exactly what part of the sky it came from it was impossible to say. It receded into pinpoint smallness and vanished in the blue. The possibility was that some kind of vessel in outer space was the source.

"Quick!" the Amazon said, glancing at Abna. "Put a detector on this ray and it'll automatically give the direction and distance of the source."

Abna leapt to the control panel and snapped the appropriate switches into commission. Outside the *Ultra* a detector aerial suddenly sprouted and began to revolve slowly, picking up the radiations from the beam and transmitting them to the reading instruments in the switchboard.… Not that Abna was watching them. He was back again at the window, watching the beam intently.

"Something's happening!" Viona said; then her voice took on an awe-struck quality. "But what?"

Nobody answered her: they were too fascinated. Attentively the four watched a curious disturbance in the chemical-compounded 'soil' at the base of the golden ray. At first it was a faint hazing of dust. Then it began to build up quickly into a series of fantastic shapes, growing ever taller. Soon a two-foot high mass of chemicals and dust was churning around in a narrow circle, always within the area of the beam. The gyrations seemed to increase somewhat and the spinning mass of chemicals became higher, and higher still, until it was not far short of five feet and a few inches in height.

"What in heaven's name is it?" the Amazon whispered.

In a few moments more she found out. The gyrating slowly ceased and the dust subsided. The spinning mystery became quite clearly revealed as a man—an old man—completely naked and rubbing his hands in his eyes as though he had been awakened from sleep.

"Who— Who is he?" stammered Viona.

"Quiet!" Abna muttered. "Let's see what happens."

CHAPTER SIX
THE SYNTHETIC PEOPLE

The ray remained undimmed, bathing the man in a curious golden glory. After a moment the man seemed to make an effort to become aware of himself. He looked about him, even toward the *Ultra*, but he did not have any chance to move toward the ship. For quite suddenly as he took an uncertain step forward, he began to fade! In a matter of seconds he had achieved complete transparency, flickered, and then vanished as though he had never been. A moment later the golden ray snapped out of existence.

Slowly the four turned and looked at one another. Then Viona blinked expressively.

"I suppose that really happened?"

"Beyond doubt," the Amazon assured her. "And I'm willing to gamble that at this moment another body, that of an unclothed and very much bemused old man, has appeared on Umnol—to grow younger henceforth. You agree, Abna?"

"Entirely. More by luck than judgment we've found out how these beings are created and—"

"Created!" Mexone exclaimed. "Did you say

created?"

"Certainly. You probably haven't grasped the link-up yet, so here it is. This planet is composed of chemicals of exactly the right type to form a human being—"

The Amazon snapped her fingers. "That's where I've seen the formula—formula for *Homo sapiens*, of course!"

"But since they are created here, out of the chemicals of the planet itself, they must be synthetic," Viona exclaimed.

"They are," the Amazon assented. "Which means, of course, that all the men and women we saw on Umnol are synthetic, and not natural people. No wonder none of them have parents, or are ever born!"

"Even so," Abna mused, "it does not account for them living backwards. That's quite a contrary effect, whether they be natural or synthetic people. It's the reason for it that stumps me."

"We'll come to that in time," the Amazon said, her interest plainly aroused by the things that had happened. "Let us examine the picture as we have it so far: a world of synthetic, backwardly living people who are not aware of their synthesis, apparently. Next, a planet close to them whereon, by very reason of its chemicals, they are created. The cause of their creation, and presumably of their disappearance to Umnol, seems to lie in that golden ray we watched. Maybe this world is only a stepping-stone to the planet we're really seeking. Abna, what are the readings on the detector?"

He walked across and studied the readings revealed

by the detector. They had stopped, stopwatch fashion, when the ray had disappeared. The Amazon moved to his side and read them with him.

"Seventy-two million miles," the Amazon said slowly. "That's a bit surprising. That beam must have been generated from seventy-two million miles away. I thought the answer lay in a space ship, but if that were the case, it would obviously move closer."

"Evidently one of the other planets in the system," Abna said. "We can soon find out which by lifting the *Ultra* into the void, and then surveying. We've found out all we need to know here—even if most of it was by accident."

No further time was wasted. Abna started up the power plant and in a moment or two the *Ultra* was dropping away into space, leaving the lavender-scented planet as a slowly decreasing ball. Here, out in free space, it was but a moment's work to detect the planet from which the golden ray had sprung.

"That one, obviously," the Amazon said, nodding towards a Martian-red point in the firmament. "It's the only planet to match the readings we took: it couldn't be any of the others because of the direction and distances." She frowned a little as she studied it, and then almost unconsciously fingered the weapons on her waist belt. "Abna, set course for that red planet."

"I'm already doing so," Abna smiled, busy at the switchboard.

"A little larger than Mars, and yet smaller than Earth," Viona said, glancing up from the instruments by which she was checking size. "Gravity slightly less than Earth, so that will give us an advantage if we think of any jumping."

"Atmosphere?" Abna questioned.

"Same as Umnol. Virtually identical, in fact."

"Good," the Amazon murmured. "That'll make breathing a bit more simple, anyway.... As for the rest," she went on, surveying the planet though the widow, "it is apparently an almost cloudless planet with a good deal of reddish soil on its surface, hence the lurid color...."

At tremendous velocity, the *Ultra* sped through the void, the distance a mere hop to its interstellar capabilities.

"How long before we land, Abna?" the Amazon asked as the planet loomed ahead of the speeding vessel.

"About forty-five minutes, allowing for deceleration."

It was some twenty minutes later with the red world leaping up at them out of the void, when something happened. All of a sudden the smooth, soundless onrush of the *Ultra* was rudely interrupted by a violent jerk. It was almost as though they had been hit by a massive meteoroid, yet nothing was visible.

"The course is deflected," Abna said grimly, swinging back into line with the planet. "Whatever hit us just then had an almighty powerful kick, considering the speed we're going at! Which reminds me! The repulsive screen isn't on. I never replaced it after we started exploring the lavender—"

He had hardly spoken before the effect came again and with much greater force. The *Ultra* checked momentarily in its hurtling onrush, lurched violently and again went off course.

"Wonder what we're hitting?" the Amazon mused, picking herself up and going to the window.

She saw only the gigantic mass of the approaching world with its patchwork quilt of surface—then yet again came the force, and this time it was overwhelming. The ship groaned under the strain then it was over. Suddenly they heard a whistling hiss.

"Air's escaping somewhere!" Abna exclaimed; then Viona pointed to a corner of the control room.

"There, Dad! Where you made that repair!"

She was right. There was a hairline fissure in the metal coated with thick frost, through which precious air was leaking into space. Evidently this one section was weak.

"Repair it," Abna said briefly. "I've got to keep my eye on the controls. We're too near the planet for me to desert them."

"Better weld it inside and out," the Amazon said, pulling out two lots of welding apparatus. "Here, Viona—you and Mexone deal with the inside. I'll tackle the outside."

In a matter of moments she was in a space suit and hurried to the upper levels of the *Ultra*, carrying the heavy welding equipment. A few minutes later she was pushing open the emergency hatch and then floated out on to the *Ultra*'s exterior, the nylon rope about her waist and affixed to the ship her only means of propulsion. Automatically by the law of mass she kept pace with the ship, but the rope enabled her to pull herself wherever she desired. Thuswise, floating in the void, she set to work with the welder, glancing at times at the gigantic world yawning some millions of miles beneath her.

As she worked she caught a brief glimpse of something intensely bright winking in the depths of the planet. It had the brilliance of an intensely powerful sun and, allowing for the distance, it was actually probably several miles wide. Only for an instant was it visible—then a few seconds later came that dreadful sense of shock.

The *Ultra* jolted as though an invisible hand had pushed it. As it shuddered and veered off-course the Amazon found herself swung clean oft the ship. Helplessly she went sailing into space, and would doubtlessly have traveled onwards at her initial velocity, had not the rope saved her. She was finally brought up with a jerk and gradually began to pull herself back, looking down at the amazing vision of the red world infinite miles beneath her feet. She was not afraid— fear was unknown to her makeup, and anyway, she had been in similar scrapes before. The one thing that interested her was that this latest onslaught had told her a good deal. She knew now just what was happening, something she could never have known while inside the ship.

Finally her job was done. The new metal and the old were flowed together and the breach sealed. She gathered up her equipment and returned through the hatch into the control room. Viona and Mexone were also at the end of their part of the task and putting the equipment away.

"Abna," the Amazon said, "switch on the invisibility screen. I think it's our only way to get out of trouble."

Abna did not ask the why or wherefore. He obeyed instantly and it seemed to the four as though they were standing in space itself with the various fittings jutting out of infinity. The explanation was simple enough. Light waves were deflected in such a manner as to prevent them illuminating the ship, thereby rendering it invisible to an onlooker, and only faintly apparent to those inside it.

CHAPTER SEVEN
THE SUPREME ONE

"Do you think this is going to do any good?" Abna inquired. "I would have done so long ago, only it occurred to me that these scientists will have detectors. They won't need to see the *Ultra* in order to attack it."

"Agreed," the Amazon assented, "but don't overlook that the deflection of light waves produces a disturbance in the immediate neighborhood—enough disturbance to prevent a detector from focusing accurately, I'm banking on that—that we'll be able to land on the planet in one piece."

Abna nodded. "Okay then—we'll try it."

"These scientists we hope shortly to meet are certainly experts," the Amazon continued, pulling off the remainder of her space suit. "Foes worthy of our steel indeed! In case you haven't realized it, they're masters of spatial-shock technique, and that's what is battering at us."

"Spatial shock?" Viona questioned. "What's that?"

"A technique which your father and I have tried to perfect and never succeeded—not because we couldn't do it, but because we never seemed to have the time.

Stated simply, it is the art of producing a ripple in the fabric of space-time. This ripple is arrow-shaped, and the point impinges on whatever object is required. In this case the object is the *Ultra*. Given the intangibility of the fabric of space-time, the scientific complication involved to produce the effect can be imagined. But it is a devastating power. Whole planets can be smashed to powder by the process. Those 'arrowed' ripples in space-time cause a gigantic shock barrier—like an invisible, impregnable wall. I figured all that out when I was swept off the *Ultra* by reason of it being taken from under my feet, and it was then that I knew only a spatial shock wave could have caused it."

"Rather like a ship being battered by a gigantic wave?" Viona mused, her scientific knowledge lagging far behind that of her phenomenal mother.

"Exactly. Only in this case these scientists are able to agitate space-time as a storm agitates the ocean." The Amazon shook her head slowly in grudging admiration. "There is science of a high order indeed!"

"Evidently it must be, to center the point of their disturbance exactly on so small a target as the *Ultra*," Abna said grimly.

The Amazon put her spacesuit and welding equipment away, then she said:

"That's why I think the invisibility will upset them. I don't think they'll be able to obtain the pinpoint definition they need from now on."

Such evidently was the case, for there were no more shock waves as they advanced, protected by their cloak of invisibility. The red world grew larger, and ever larger, the *Ultra*'s speed constantly dropping—until at last clear outlines on the surface of the planet became visible. Here it was that the watching Crusaders received their first surprise. What they had at first mistaken for soil—for they had not made a telescopic observation—was actually nothing of the kind. The redness was caused by buildings—tens of thousands of them—covering almost every portion of the planet's surface. The buildings were nearly all of the skyscraper design, and they gave the impression of forming one planet-wide city so closely were they interlinked.

"From the look of things," Abna said, "they seem to be pushed for room down there. Like some of our countries back on Earth, they've had to build upwards instead of sideways."

Abna's main concern was in finding a clear spot to land, so close were the edifices huddled together. Eventually he detected a small, park-like space that was apparently deserted, so he quickly made for it and, by dint of considerable maneuvering, managed to land. Even then there was only just space for the huge vessel to fit.

"How about the invisibility?" Abna asked, as he cut off the power plant.

"Better come back to normal," the Amazon decided. "Now we are here we'll be detected, invisibility or otherwise, so there doesn't seem much point in concealing ourselves."

Abna nodded and moved the required switches. Instantly the *Ultra* assumed its normal solid form. This done, Abna crossed to the observation window. He stood gazing outside, the Amazon, Viona, and Mexone beside him. Up to now there were no signs of life as far as people were concerned, but in the near distance the red city was visible, aircraft going and coming, and the busy, high-flung vehicular traffic ways crowded with machines going to and fro. The whole impression conveyed was one of some super-anthill working at full capacity.

Out of nowhere merged three men, and within seconds they were completely substantial.

The Amazon held her fire even though her gun was out of her belt and at the ready. Abna just stood as he was, waiting for whatever should happen next—and at the same time extracting quite a deal of interest from his study of these beings of the mysterious red planet.

They were men, no doubt of that, but of rather curious build. In height none of them was above four feet, and yet they were immensely broad-shouldered and solid-looking. They gave all the indications of possessing colossal strength despite their lack of height. They were dressed in one-piece uniforms and bore some kind of odd insignia on their right sleeves. About their almost non-existent waists were belts of a glittering silvery metal, which carried a variety of weapons. One of the weapons, a wicked looking, oddly designed gun, which was in each of their hands at the moment, steadily pointed.

Such were the outer details—but the attention was automatically drawn to the faces. They were so completely square as it is possible for a human face to be, with thin nose and rat-trap mouth. The eyes were bigger than is common to a human being, very round and with scarlet irises, which gave a horribly sinister impression—an effect heightened by the tremendous foreheads and complete lack of hair.

The two groups stared at each other.

"Can you understand this language?" Abna asked at last, and the reply came so suddenly that he started.

"Certainly we can understand it. We knew every detail of your language, your clumsy science, and your purpose within a few seconds of meeting you face to face...." It was the third man who was talking, every word rapped out with a vicious distinctness, and his thin lips shutting tight during the pauses.

"From which," Abna remarked dryly, "I assume that we are not welcome here?"

"That should have been apparent by our efforts to destroy you while you were in space—and that we would have done had you not resorted to invisibility. No matter—you merely postponed the issue. We shall—"

The man stopped suddenly as something on his belt began to buzz softly. He lifted up from the belt an instrument that was obviously a minute television receiver, no bigger than a small pocket watch. Adjusting it, he watched and listened. By some curious system of amplification a voice spoke at full power, in an unknown language, and a tiny face appeared on the little viewing screen. The man stiffened.

"Our original orders were to destroy you," he said curtly. "Now you have been observed, heard, and studied by the Supreme One, the orders have been countermanded. He desires audience with you immediately. Come!"

The man turned and then hesitated as the four made no effort to move.

"I had overlooked that you are not exponents of the fourth dimension," he said cynically. "Open the airlock and pass to the outside at once."

Abna looked at the Amazon and she gave a shrug.

"We're in it, Abna: we might as well finish it."

Abna snapped a switch and watched the huge airlock open ponderously; then he turned as the third man spoke again.

"Do not waste your time closing the door again after you have passed to the outside. It will do you no good. Walls are not a barrier to us."

Uncomfortably aware of the truth of this, Abna led the way outside with the Amazon immediately behind him. More slowly came Viona and Mexone, their eyes on the stocky, powerful men who had captured them.

From the park-like area the journey led across a bridge set high above surging, strangely-designed traffic. Then from the bridge the party found themselves walking into a huge, cage-like affair with a metal grille for a door. The Amazon, looking down between her feet, saw a dizzying depth of nearly 1,000 feet where people moved like specks and vehicles had assumed toy size. Apparently the park, the bridge, and the cage were all far above the city proper, or else great portions of the city were nearly subterranean.

"Stand still and wait!" ordered the third man.

The four did as ordered, watching as the three guards came close to them and also stood waiting. The reason became apparent when from somewhere above a shaft of vermilion-tinted light enveloped them—and instantly they began to rise in defiance of gravity, up and up through the towering cage to a height of 500 feet above their former level.

"An elevator without ropes or floor," the Amazon commented, intrigued. "These people are certainly scientists, whatever else they might be."

Scarlet eyes turned to her, but no comment was made. The mysterious levitating beam extinguished itself when the four were standing on yet another grating floor at the cage tower summit. Ahead of them was a thin bridge of metal, stretching over the skyscraper roofs. To any person suffering from fear of heights, such a view would have produced complete collapse.

It was plain that the Amazon had reached the limit of her patience. Where Abna was disposed to see what happened, the Amazon was not. It went against her individual nature to be treated as a captive—and accordingly she suddenly stopped her advance, while Abna went on. In a moment Viona and Mexone caught up with her.

"What's the matter?" Viona asked. "Surely you're not afraid to go on?"

"Hardly," the Amazon returned dryly. "Both of you squeeze past me, and keep going."

It was not so easy within the narrow limits of the bridge, but gradually it was accomplished, leaving the Amazon isolated from the others and facing the guards. Her proton gun leaped suddenly into her hand as they came toward her.

"Why have you stopped?" the leader demanded, his red eyes fixed on the proton gun, "Continue immediately!"

"On one condition," the Amazon replied. "I will continue with my colleagues to the abode of the Supreme One if I am permitted to do so without escort. Otherwise I'll not go. I refuse to have dealings with underlings: only with superiors."

For answer the guard leveled his own weapon menacingly and his finger curled around the trigger. It was an action that required only seconds, but the Amazon was ahead of those seconds. She did not know what was intended, nor did she wait to see. She hurled herself forward along the narrow length and brought her gun-fist down on the guard's wrist before he could complete his actions. Instantly he gave a howl of pain as bone cracked under the splintering force of the blow.

Without hesitating a moment the Amazon seized the guard around the waist, heaved him into the air—a simple task in so light a gravity—and then flung him outwards into space. He went down instantly into the yawning canyon of the city.

Swaying dizzily on the narrow bridge, the Amazon

fell on her knees, and that unintentional action undoubtedly saved her a good deal of trouble as the other guards fired. Green rays from their guns shot over the Amazon's head and melted the metalwork of the bridge wherever they touched.

In another moment she had her own gun level, only to have it kicked out of her hand by the nearest guard. But he wasn't quick enough. The Amazon's hand seized his outflung ankle and with a vicious twist she flung him off his feet.

He dropped, half off the bridge and bent backwards. In another moment his legs had slid over the edge, too, and he went hurtling down after his comrade. The Amazon stayed as she was on her knees, deprived of her gun and watching the remaining guard coming slowly toward her. Apparently his gun had to undergo a brief pause after firing a charge, for as he moved forward he operated a thin rod on the side of the gun, which, presumably, activated it to firing point again.

But the Amazon did not wait for this. She sprang to her feel abruptly and, again taking advantage of the light gravity, catapulted herself forward and came to grips with the man even as he struggled with his gun. Instantly he dropped the gun and his arms came around the bottom of the Amazon's back with a terrific, spine-cracking pressure. For the first time the Amazon realized that she was encountering somebody as strong, and even stronger, than herself. It was a test of muscles now—not guns.

Back along the bridge Abna, Viona, and Mexone

returned slowly to watch what was happening. Mexone yanked out his gun and tried to aim it, until Abna's hand held his arm.

"Don't try," he cautioned. "They're too close together. I fancy she'll be able to take care of herself."

Abna had hardly spoken before the guard suddenly relinquished his bear-hug. Indeed he had to do so to save his neck being broken—and that was the Amazon's chance. She abruptly changed her tactics and lashed out a smashing blow straight into the guard's stomach. Breath belched out of him in an explosion of wind and he doubled in anguish—then he flattened as a yellow fist crashed down on the back of his neck at the base of the skull. Senseless, he dropped face down on the bridge and, for a second or two, the Amazon stood breathing hard and looking at him—then her eyes rose to Abna, Viona, and Mexone beyond him.

"Give me your gun, Mexone; I'll probably have more need to use it than you. Mine's gone for good."

He handed it over and she clutched it tightly in her hand, her face grim.

"All right," she said curtly. "Now let ns see this egotistical being who calls himself the Supreme One."

Squeezing past Abna, she led the party thereafter, coming finally to the end of the bridge. It terminated in a massive red metal door, which mysteriously opened as the four slowly and warily came up to it.

"Do we risk it?" the Amazon asked, glancing about her.

"We've not much choice," Abna responded.

They looked around them again, loath to take the final step. They surveyed the infinity of red buildings, the awful drop beneath their feet, and then looked into the cool length of hall of this lonely eyrie far above the city. They had made a promise to the people of Umnol: they must do their utmost to keep it.

They had only moved a few yards down the hall; then, to their amazement, the floor suddenly began moving forward towards an open doorway at the far end.

"Hang on," Abna murmured. "Moving floor to carry us to our destination, I imagine."

He was right. In a few moments the moving floor had taken them through the distant doorway into the center of a large room. It looked rather like a lounge, with very normal chairs and articles of furniture in various positions. Dominant about the room was a gigantic window, giving a breathtaking view of the city in all directions.

The door shut abruptly of its own accord. There was nobody in sight. Only the cold, impersonal walls quite tastefully decorated. The Amazon made to move forward but to her surprise she was literally rooted to the spot. In fact they all were.

"Very interesting," Abna murmured. "Magnetism. Evidently the Supreme One intends to make sure we stay put."

"Well, we have our guns anyway," the Amazon said grimly; then she turned sharply as a panel of the wall shot up. There was a brief vision of vast, brightly lighted instruments in the room beyond, then one of the square, massive-shouldered men of the planet came into view and the panel closed behind him.

The quartet returned stare for stare as the man's boring eyes surveyed them. Each of them experienced the almost uncanny hypnotic force that the man exerted—but their minds were proof against the onslaught, even though the effort was considerable.

"I am interested, my friends, in meeting you face to face at last," the man said presently, coming forward slowly. "Up to now I have watched and listened to you by instruments"—he nodded toward the room from which he had come—"which, however efficient, can never equal the real thing. You will forgive the precaution of the magnetized floor? You know, of course, who I am?"

"The Supreme One, ruler of this planet," Abna said.

"Exactly—and that position carries a great deal of responsibility, as you may imagine. The kind of responsibility which I do not like having disturbed by four cranks from the depths of space!"

The scarlet eyes smoldered in sudden venom, and once again the four found themselves combating the waves of hatred which were hurled at them. Then gradually the miasma faded.

"I know all about you, and your avocation of helping backward races on whatever worlds you happen to come across. Why you should concern yourselves is none of my business, I admit. But it is my business when you decide to investigate the circumstances underlying the world of Umnol. Why did you take such a task unto yourselves?"

"A world which lives backwards is hardly one to be passed over lightly," Abna said. "We were—and still are—curious as to the reason. Even more so the reason for people who live their lives grave to cradle— speaking in the wide sense, that is. We have solved part of the mystery in discovering that the people are synthetic: we have yet to puzzle out the remainder."

"I sense considerable contempt in your minds— contempt for me, my world, and my accomplishments. Others have expressed similar contempt among my own people, and have died because of it. I see no reason why you, complete strangers, should be exempt. That you have come from a far-distant world is very inter- esting, but not interesting enough to make me wish to receive you as friends. You are enemies in that you have dared to interest yourselves in the paradoxical world of Umnol.... On the other hand, I admire your courage in so tampering with that which you do not understand—a courage further exemplified in the way you attacked the guards with only a slender bridge between you and death."

"At least give us the chance to discuss," Abna suggested, conscious of approaching danger. "We have perhaps more in common with you than—"

The Supreme One came forward at that, his merci- less eyes glowing.

"I will show you the quality of the mind-science you are trying feebly to fight," he said coldly. "Before

I part from you let me comfort you with a thought. Your space machine is—or soon will be—destroyed, so even if you should escape the crushing prison I am about to build for you, it will do you no good. Behold, then, my power!"

Abruptly he put his feet a little apart and clenched his hands at his sides, throwing all the power of his highly trained mind into a sudden tremendous effort. Under the force of his battering mental waves the four swayed helplessly, their senses swimming. For a moment or two they could not fight back against the hypnotic torrent. And even when they did force themselves to somewhat control the situation, they realized that the lounge had disappeared. Instead they were surrounded with rock walls—rock ceiling—rock floor. Mysteriously, they were inside a mass of rock, and yet illumination was there with no explanation as to its source.

"Where are we?" Mexone panted, looking about him. "What's that devil done?"

"The magnetism's gone anyway," the Amazon said, moving her feet freely. "But that doesn't explain how we come to be in this cavern, or cave, or whatever it is. And where does the light come from? We're in another space, of course, and that might account for transmitting light four-dimensionally, but even so I don't—"

"These walls, and the ceiling, are moving inwards!" Abna interrupted, his voice taut.

The Amazon, Víona, and Mexone turned and watched intently, and the horror of the situation became immediately evident to them. Without a sound the walls were coming nearer, and also the ceiling—while the rock floor seemed to remain stationary.

"Wait a minute!" Abna exclaimed, his eyes brightening, "I think I have the answer. It isn't really happening. It's an illusion—the power of mental suggestion."

"Granting you're right," Viona said, "how do we beat it?"

"Deny its existence until our minds become cleared of the illusion and cease to accept it—then it will vanish. That's the basis of all mind-science. And remember, a mental suggestion can only suggest: it can never prove itself, because it doesn't exist. Concentrate—as never before."

They fell silent, convinced that Abna had the right answer. Nevertheless it demanded tremendous self-control to stand still and watch the walls contract, at the same time mentally denying their existence. It was a silent battle—a battle between the implanted mental suggestion of the Supreme One and the four mentally adroit Crusaders.

And, suddenly, the illusion vanished! They were still in the lounge of the eyrie. The only difference was that the magnetism had gone from the floor, and of the Supreme One there was no sign. The panel through which he had originally appeared was adamantly closed.

CHAPTER EIGHT
BATTLE IN THE ARENA

"Then I was right," Abna commented, looking about him. "There never was a contracting rock: it was all mental suggestion, which pursued to its final limits would have killed."

"But where's the Supreme One?" the Amazon demanded. "Surely he ought to have waited to see the consummation of his efforts?"

"Looks to me like a case of underestimating the enemy," Viona commented. "He was so sure the hypnotic suggestion would work that he didn't wait until the finish—fortunately for us."

"It's the only answer," Abna agreed. "And we'd better start moving fast before those instruments of his tell him we're still going strong. Let's get back to the *Ultra*. Once inside it we can map out a proper plan of attack, knowing the nature of the enemy."

Without further hesitation they turned to the door by which they had entered. It was, of course, locked, and all their efforts failed to budge it.

"The window," the Amazon said quickly. "It's our only means of exit."

No difficulty presented itself here. It was partly open anyway—one huge pane revolving on pivots. To open it still wider and slide outside on to a narrow ledge of red masonry presented no trouble. The most difficult part was to inch around gradually to the front of the building, with only the narrow ledge as support. Backs to the wall, moving carefully, with a 1,000-foot abyss before them, the four gradually progressed—until at last they gained the safety of the front steps.

"There'll probably be fun and games on the way back to the *Ultra*," Abna said. "Anyway, we've got guns—and we'll use them if we have to."

At that he started forward along the treacherously narrow bridge, then almost immediately stopped again as he noticed a figure approaching along it, very slowly and painfully.

"It's that guard you knocked out!" Abna said abruptly. "I didn't notice him before: he must have just stood up."

"And he's in our way," the Amazon said grimly.

The Amazon fired, and devastating force of the protonic gun did its work instantly. The guard simply vanished in a puff of smoke and intense blue-white flame—but at the same instant something else happened. The bridge swayed violently and then sagged.

"Your gun's cut the bridge through!" Abna gasped, then before he could say anything else he went plunging downwards as the bridge snapped.

The Amazon, Viona, and Mexone went down, too,

clinging to the bridge with all their strength. It had now become a twisted rope ladder of snapped cables and severed meshwork. Almost at its extremity the four clung for their lives, swaying far above the roofs of the city.

"Climb up," Abna said, muscling himself a little higher. "Nothing else we can do."

"No—wait a minute." Clinging with one hand, the Amazon looked below her at the roofs; then she said: "There is a roof there—see it? About fifty feet below us and taller than all the others. Sort of tower thing. Suppose we try to reach it? It we go up, we've no way out. It's a blind alley."

"You propose to drop fifty feet without trouble?" Abna questioned.

"I don't know, but the gravity is less than normal, and I prefer the risk to being in the hands of the Supreme One. I'm going to take the chance."

She swung herself gently to and fro, aiming for position. It had to be dead correct. If she missed, she would hurtle down the full distance to certain death. Then, timing herself, she let go her hold and flew outwards and downwards. The fall seemed never-ending, but with the lesser gravity she had the chance of somewhat directing her movement. The flat roof shot out of the depths and she hit it on the very edge with all the breath knocked out of her. Slowly she clawed her way forward and then stood up and waved an arm reassuringly.

Abna came next, and then Mexone. Both arrived

with several inches to spare, but Viona was not so lucky. She just missed the roof edge, and would have gone hurtling into the depths had not the Amazon grabbed her wrist and jerked her upwards. Shaky and out of breath, Viona tossed back the fallen copper hair from her face.

"Thanks!" she panted. "That's one trapeze act I wouldn't like to do again."

"Queer we're not being molested," Abna frowned. "I should have thought that by this time the Supreme One would have realized things are not as they should be—"

"We'll have time enough to worry about him when we've got to," the Amazon interrupted. "We want to get hack to the *Ultra*—and quick. Better go over the roofs in the general direction of the broken bridge end—the other end, I mean. That should be a guide for us."

So, keeping the view of the broken bridge constantly ahead of them, they set off again across the highest city roofs, on quite one of the most hair-raising trips they had ever made.

"Look!" the Amazon said suddenly, as they hesitated before a leap to yet another building.

The others followed the direction she indicated. From here they were looking down into a 1,000-foot depth. At the base of it was a street, and along it marched a small army of men and women, all clad in a drab blue uniform, while on either side of them paraded perhaps six guards.

"Prisoners," Abna murmured, gazing. "Or something like it. Look at the way they move—they drag along: they don't march. And those are guards all right: we can recognize them by this time."

"There's something extremely rotten about the set-up on this planet," the Amazon said grimly, "and before we're through we'll probably find out what it is."

They had covered perhaps five roofs, and were not far from the bridge 'sign post' when Abna stopped again and motioned the others. He was looking down through a metal grating set in the roof, his face grim.

"A bit more of the stuff that makes this planet horrible," he said grimly. "Look at this—"

The others gazed down, and their first reaction was of intense anger against the Supreme One, whom they assumed was responsible. Through the grating, which was evidently some kind of ventilator, they could distinguish men and women in the last stages of starvation.

"Notice something about them?" Viona asked suddenly. "They look like us. They are not bald, for one thing, and I'll swear they haven't got red eyes. Then again, they're about normal height."

"I believe you're right," Abna agreed, studying them. "That seems to indicate that the red-eyed eyed ones are a different race, or something."

"I'll make a guess and say of a different planet," the Amazon added; then her tone changed. "Anyway, this is one job we have got to do. *Ultra* or no *Ultra*. Make a way of escape for these folks."

"They'll only be recaptured," Abna said, thinking.

"That's up to them. Once they have their freedom, and in quantity, there's no telling what they'll do."

Quite decided on her course of action, the Amazon went to work. Whipping out her proton gun she screwed the nozzle firing-point to its smallest capacity, and then projected a hair-thin stream of destructive energy at the edge of the ventilator grating. In a moment the metal smoked, turned white hot, then passed into vapor. It was only the work of perhaps five minutes to cut the tough metal all around and lift the grating aside.

Bewildered, the men and women watched as the Amazon leaped down lithely into their midst.

"Outside," she said, motioning. "Every one of you. Make your own way of escape."

Possibly they understood; possibly they didn't—but they knew that somebody was trying to help them, and once they reached the freedom of the exterior there was a good deal they could do. Abna dropped down a moment later and between them he and the Amazon lifted each prisoner into the waiting hands of Viona and Mexone—and so one by one all the living ones were removed.

When the last one was out the Amazon surveyed the stinking, metal-walled chamber with disgust. There was nothing left in it now except corpses. Those who had found escape were already looking for, and finding, emergency ladders down from the roof.

"Up to them now," the Amazon said at length. Then she considered. "This seems to be some kind of prison. Maybe there are others in difficulty. Do we look?"

"Might as well," Mexone said. "Let's finish what we've started."

The Amazon turned her gun on the metal door, widening the firing nozzle to the limit. There was a blast of flame, a brief shock wave, and the solid metal ceased to be. Through the acrid-smelling, dispersing haze a long metal corridor was revealed beyond, lined on each side with cell doors. Plainly the place was a prison, though there were no signs of guards as yet.

"Let's go," the Amazon said briefly, leading the way. She strode forward into the corridor, stopping at the first door, to find it solid—as indeed were all the doors. She only hesitated for a moment, then again operated her proton gun and set the door swinging wide. There was not the time to see who was imprisoned within, so she and the others made a routine ceremony of blasting open every one of the doors as they passed them, and then continuing into the narrow corridor beyond. It traveled a fair distance and turned an abrupt corner.

"They're beginning to come out of those cells behind us," Viona said, glancing back. "Men and women, about in the last stages of exhaustion."

The Amazon nodded briefly. "Up to them now: we've done what we can, Surprising thing to me is that there are no guards on duty—"

She had just spoken when a guard appeared around the corner they were approaching. He appeared to have come up a flight of stairs. He stopped dead—one of the short, red-eyed men—staring at the advancing four, and that moment of uncertainty gave the Amazon the advantage. She did not use her gun but instead leaped forward with the speed of a panther, drew hack her right fist, then smashed it clean into the guard's face.

"Keep him quiet for a while anyway," the Amazon said. "Wonder where he was making for?"

"Probably the prisons—" Abna broke off and looked suddenly ahead as there came a sudden roar of voices, remarkably like those at an exciting open-air meeting.

"Sounds odd," the Amazon said. "We'd better look."

They raced along the short length to the open doorway from which the sounds had come—and the scene that burst upon them was reminiscent of something taken from the archives of ancient Rome.

There was a big indoor amphitheater, lighted by concealed illumination. Around the amphitheater were the square-shouldered, stocky, red-eyed men in their hundreds—bald and intent. Nowhere was there a sign of a woman. It was exactly like a circus arena surrounded by spectators who were all identical. The exact purpose of this strange business became apparent a moment later as a young girl was led into view. She was one of the 'normal' race, with long, trailing fair hair and almost threadbare garments. Perhaps she was sixteen, and in the last stages of terror and exhaustion. Her limbs, plentifully on view, were bony to the point of emaciation. On cither side of her, holding her arms fiercely, were two of the red-eyed guards.

"There's something about this I don't like," the Amazon said; her eyes glinting. "In fact, I don't like anything about this planet."

"This evidently is where all the guards are," Abna said. "Watching this business. The one we saw was probably coming to get more victims for—"

He broke off, his hand tightening on the Amazon's arm. Into the ring had come something else—an animal of some kind. It was something between a tiger and a lion, but a good deal bigger, and possessing one enormous tearing fang in its upper jaw. There was no doubt it was a member of the cat family from the way it loped into view, its enormous green eyes fixed on the solitary girl. Then came another of the animals—and another. Until at least four of them were circling the girl slowly.

"The filthy lot of fiends!" Viona exclaimed suddenly. "One girl against four monsters like that doesn't stand a ghost of a chance."

The Amazon hesitated for a moment, then she carefully adjusted her gun and leveled it toward the prowling beasts.

"We're not dead yet, Abna, and I for one am not leaving that youngster to the mercies of these sadists."

With that she sighted carefully, then fired. One of the huge beasts, just in the act of padding toward girl, received the full blast of the weapon and disappeared in a blinding flash of flame. The bald-heads rose to their feet in furious amazement, and the girl herself glanced about her in bewilderment.

In general, the effect was not what the Amazon intended, for the remaining three beasts, thinking that the girl herself was somehow responsible for the disappearance of one of their number, turned on her with slavering jaws.

"Now what?" Abna asked tautly. "They're too close for any firing. It'll kill the girl as well."

The Amazon put her gun away and instead pulled out a short, needle-thin knife. She put it between her teeth and then let her next actions be her answer. In one leap she was over the low fence at the edge of the ring and speeding in great leaps toward the petrified youngster.

What the bald-heads thought of the business there wasn't time to find out. At the moment they were gazing in stupefaction at the black-clad, superbly modeled woman who had mysteriously come on to the scene—then their eyes jerked to the mighty form of Abna, and the agile Viona and Mexone coming behind him, as they too, abandoned hiding and leaped to the attack.

Though she never shifted her vision, the Amazon was aware of Abna, Viona, and Mexone all circling carefully, holding themselves ready for attack at any moment. Their main idea was to get out of the ring, or fire at the brute at a convenient moment—but such a plan was by no means easy to put into effect. Further, the girl had to be rescued, too.

It was the brute nearest the Amazon that broke the stalemate. It leaped suddenly, its vast claws outspread. At the same second the Amazon leaped too, and, aided by the lesser gravity, she sailed over the flying monster's head and landed behind it. It came to a baffled stop, snarling, smothered in the dust it had plowed up. It turned its head, and the Amazon charged straight at it and landed astride its back, driving her thin-bladed knife into its muscular body. She stabbed as fast as she could, trusting to luck to find a vital spot, for she had no idea of the creature's anatomy

It reared, lashed, and screamed in fury, as the knife bit to the hilt each time. The Amazon held on with her left hand, her fingers under the massive throat. But savagely and blindly though she stabbed, she seemed unable to find a vital spot—then suddenly she was flung from the creature's back, her knife sailing into the air.

Even as she landed on her back the beast plunged after her. Automatically she threw up her hands and they sank deeply into the powerful neck. Somehow, exerting all her strength, she held away the snarling jaws striving to close on her head and face. Meantime, the claws of the brute ripped at her body and legs, inflicting deep gashes.

The others could not help her. They, too, were involved in a life and death struggle, in which the nearness of the attack prevented the use of guns. The Amazon realized she had only her own ingenuity and superhuman strength to rely upon—and she exerted both to the full because she had to.

As she strove with all her power to keep the head away, she lifted her torn and lacerated legs and doubled them up so that finally her feet pressing under the brute's stomach. Then, choosing the right moment, she used her leg muscles with all their power, releasing her hold on the brute's neck at the same moment. Impelled by her enormous strength, rendered all the greater by the friendly gravity, the beast was flung upwards and outwards for a distance of six feet. In those split seconds the Amazon wrenched out her gun and aimed it.

She was a fraction too slow. The instant the beast dropped it twirled hack to the attack. A mighty claw ripped the Amazon's arm from shoulder to wrist, tearing the gun out of her hand and filling her with tearing pain. Again the head snapped down, the fighting fang striving to gouge at her, but she twisted desperately and missed the main onslaught.

Then suddenly her grip slipped and she crashed on her back in the dust. The brute reared its head and she closed her eyes for the final blow of the deadly fang that would undoubtedly finish her.… Instead there was a puff of strong wind and a slight shock wave. Then a smell of burning flesh and hair.

Amazed, she opened her eyes. She beheld the much-shaken figure of the young girl, holding the proton gun and staring in fascination at the spot where the beast had been. Then she suddenly came to herself and hurried to the spot where the Amazon was lying. She held down a thin, delicate hand to help her rise, and with an effort the Amazon got to her feet.

"Good girl," she murmured thankfully, taking the gun—then, trying hard to combat the pain she was experiencing she moved to where Abna, Viona, and

Mexone were fighting with knives and muscles to kill the remaining two beasts.

"Get clear!" the Amazon shouted. "All of you—get clear!"

No questions were asked: they never were in an emergency. By slow degrees the trio disentangled themselves from the two creatures—then when the moment was propitious the Amazon fired her gun relentlessly. The outcome was obvious. First one brute vanished into thin air, then the remaining one followed it. There was only the smoke and dust left in the air as a dense pall.

"Get out quick!" the Amazon panted. "To escape the bald-heads. Our only chance!"

She raced across to the solitary girl and grabbed her. Then they all five hurtled back in the direction they had come—into the prison passage, shielded for the most part by the fog of dust and dispersing smoke. Shouts they could hear in plenty, becoming more clamorous as they blundered up the short passage, then up the stairway—and so to the prison cell corridor and finally the big cell with its open ventilator.

No words were passed. Abna leaped up to the opening first and then lifted the wondering girl captive up behind him. Viona, the Amazon, and lastly Mexone followed.

"This will slow 'em up," Abna said, and whirled the ventilator grille back in place, welding the edges with his flame gun.

"What now?" Viona panted, looking about her.

"The *Ultra*, of course—as we originally intended," the Amazon said. "And we'll have to be quick. I'm beginning to feel weak through losing so much blood."

Abna glanced at her still-bleeding, badly-torn arm, and the remnants of fabric clinging to her lacerated legs.

"No time now for metaphysical concentration to put you right," he said. "Only answer is let me carry you!"

"Carry me!" The Amazon looked indignant and desperately tired at the same time. "Never—"

"We're not going to leave you, and your slowness may hinder us all," Abna pointed out. "Please do it, Vi, and forget your pride for once."

As it happened the issue decided itself for, unexpectedly, the Amazon suddenly collapsed to the roof. Instantly Abna picked up her unconscious form and perched her across his shoulders.

"Tie her hands to her feet," he instructed Viona. "She won't slip in the leaps we'll have to make. And you'll have to help our young friend as best you can."

Viona did as she was bidden, using the emergency nylon cord from her belt. It took her only a few minutes, but by the time she had finished there came distinct shouts and cries of fury from somewhere below the ventilator.

"The bald-heads," Abna said briefly. "Time we went."

He raced to the edge of the parapet and measured the distance to the next nearest roof—then he took the leap, fully aware of the risk with the Amazon's dead weight across his shoulders. But he managed success-fully—as also did Viona, with the girl slave clinging for dear life to her back. Then came Mexone, his gun in readiness if any bald-heads showed up in the rear.

So, by degrees, the journey over the roofs to the point where the bridge began was completed. The fugitives surveyed the smashed structure hanging down, then looked beyond it.

"There's the cage that carried us up," Viona said, pointing. "And there's the bottom of it."

She indicated its base far below the level of the roof on which they now stood. Taking the base as their point of observation they followed it until they beheld the original normal bridge they had crossed, and beyond that again the park-like area. There, dimly visible in the distance, was the *Ultra*—but there were small figures moving industriously about it.

Abna fell silent, considering the latticed metal struc-ture sweeping 500 feet down into the lower quarters of the city. They had come up it by some remote-controlled levitation—but how to get down it?

"Only one way," he said, following his own thoughts, "and that is to climb down—and to leap from this roof to there is going to be some job."

"We've got this far," Viona said confidently. "We can finish it."

"Spoken like a true daughter," Abna smiled; then hitching the Amazon more firmly on to his shoulders he measured his distance—and leaped.

Down he went, and because of the lesser gravity the

fall seemed to be never-ending. For several seconds he had the fear that he had underestimated the distance due to the Amazon's extra weight, but this proved to be merely an illusion as he beheld the huge levitation cage flying up to meet him. He reached out his hands and hit the metalwork violently, clinging on.

After that the rest was not particularly difficult, since in the metalwork there was plenty of toe and finger holds. He went down hand over hand, noticing that immediately above him Viona had arrived safely with the slave girl clinging tightly to her back. Farther up still was Mexone.

It was the work of perhaps fifteen seconds to complete the descent. Coming together into a small group, they surveyed. Ahead of them was the short bridge that vaulted over the city to the park-like area beyond, where lay the *Ultra*—figures still moving busily around it.

"We've no time to parley or ask questions," Abna said finally. "We'll blast our way through. Come on."

His gun ready in his hand, Abna led the advance. Mexone was right behind him, using the gun he had taken from the Amazon's belt. Viona, too, was armed, one hand holding on to the arm of the slave girl as she hurried her along.

The bridge was soon crossed—all of them wondering how they managed to elude capture for so long—then as they came within full view of the *Ultra* they were abruptly sighted. The half-dozen bald-heads going in and out of the airlock stopped in their activities and pointed.

"Let them have it," Abna said briefly. "There's no other way."

He was only just in time. Three of the guards had whipped out their own guns even as a shaft of devastating fire leaped toward them. Instantly one of them vanished, in the usual smoke and brilliant flame. With Mexone and Viona also firing the job was soon done. In less than thirty seconds there were no guards left.

"Ruthless, but necessary," Abna commented, slipping his gun back in his belt. "Let's see what damage they've done."

He led the way into the control room and looked about him. There was no sign of actual damage, but on the floor was a piece of stiff parchment-like paper, covered with designing. At a glance Abna saw what it was, and smiled grimly.

"So they were in the midst of making a diagram of the power plant," he commented. "Evidently the *Ultra*'s system of space travel is something new to this crowd."

Going across to the wall couch, he carefully laid the Amazon down upon it; then he moved to the switchboard. First he closed the airlock, then he applied just enough power to lift the vessel nearly 100 miles into the sky, dropping into a low orbit about the planet below.

"Since our friends seem able to walk through repulsive screens and walls, this is probably the best deterrent," he said; then with a glance at the Amazon he added: "Now leave me to deal with your mother,

Viona. Take this slave girl along with you and fit her out in decent clothes. We'll talk later.… Mexone, keep on the watch by the observation window and at the first sign of trouble let me know."

Orders were obeyed immediately; then left comparatively to himself Abna sat down beside the wall couch and, by degrees, transferred himself into one of those strange metaphysical trances of which he was superbly capable under pressure. With nothing to disturb him, his work had instant results.

Before his eyes the savage lacerations on the Amazon's limbs began to heal, and within five minutes new flesh had formed. With it came slowly returning consciousness, and at last the Amazon opened her deep violet eyes and gazed in vague wonder.

"Better?" Abna inquired, relaxing into his normal self.

"Yes, I'm better." The Amazon looked around her and then slowly sat up and held her forehead. "What happened, anyway—? Oh, yes, I remember! The tiger animals! I passed out."

"Exactly, but you're all right now. You know how these things are dealt with. Metaphysical process. You might have been in pretty bad shape if I hadn't gone to work on you."

The Amazon gave one of her rare smiles and patted Abna's hand.

"Thanks, Abna," she said quietly. "Don't think I'm not grateful. I don't quite know how you do these things, but thanks again all the same."

She got to her feet, flexing her arms and legs. Then when she reached the observation window she paused in surprise.

"We're in space!"

Abna nodded. "I thought it safer, considering we're dealing with gentlemen who walk through walls. That slave girl's being looked after by Viona, and— Ah! Here she is now!"

He and the Amazon watched with interest as the slave girl preceded Viona into the control room—and there was little doubt that Viona had done a good job. While nothing could disguise the young woman's emaciation, cosmetics, a modern hair-do, and fresh clothes—albeit of the Crusader variety—had transformed the wretched little slave into a shy, passably pretty girl with curly fair hair.

"Naturally," the Amazon said, crossing over to her, "you don't understand our language?"

The girl stared with wide blue eyes, trying to comprehend; at which the Amazon glanced at Abna.

"Better give her a course of the educator," he said, and went over to the instrument in question.

Having complete trust in her rescuers the girl did everything they indicated, seating herself before the machine and submitting quite passively to having the transmission helmet fixed over her head. Thereafter, as the power was applied, she sat like one in a dream as language, knowledge, and scientific facts were poured into her brain and automatically assimilated.... At the end of ten minutes Abna switched off and smiled.

"Quite happy?" he inquired, removing the helmet, and the girl smiled back at him.

"Yes, Abna of Jupiter—quite happy." She spoke in a soft, melodious voice in keeping with her elfin appearance. "I am thinking of the wonder of being able to talk your language and, partly, understand your science. But then, you are all miracle workers! But a while ago, before I was given these new clothes, I saw you"—she looked at the Amazon—"on the point of death from injuries from the extads. Yet now you are normal. Only miracle workers could bring about such cures."

"Not miracle workers—just scientists," Abna said. "And we are your friends. Realize that."

"I do realize it—and it is a wonderful thing to have such friends when the Mithons dominate my planet and enslave my race."

"The Mithons, I take it, are the red-eyed race?" the Amazon asked. "And the extads will be the animals from which we rescued you?"

"That is so."

"And your name?" Abna inquired.

"My name is Naisoom—Jalen Naisoom. I am the daughter of one of the high officials of our world, only—" The girl's eyes began to mist and she averted her head. "I—I saw him killed in the arena by the extads some days ago, at the order of the Mithons."

The Amazon moved forward and put a protecting arm about the girl's shoulders.

"We understand your grief, Jalen. Cry if you want to: at least it may relieve you.... Here, come into a more comfortable chair and rest while we get a meal together."

She raised the girl to her feet, took her over to one of the more comfortable chairs, and there left her to regain control of her emotions. By the time she had done so the four Crusaders had washed and changed and a meal was ready.... With a serious little smile of thanks, Jalen joined them.

CHAPTER NINE
PLANS OF THE MITHONS

During the course of the meal, at which Jalen ate voraciously, the Amazon explained matters in detail and came right up-to-date. Without interruption Jalen listened, able to understand everything that had been told her, thanks to the transference of knowledge and language.

"So that is the situation," the Amazon finished. "The World of Umnol is cursed with reversing life. In between is a lethal, lavender-scented planet where synthetic beings are created, and last of all is this planet of yours, where lies the answer to everything.… What is its name, by the way?"

"We call it Dard," Jalen said. "Not so very long ago it was a very happy planet, and the people were prosperous. They were various countries, even as there seem to be on your own far-flung world of Earth. Then came the dreaded Mithons. With their scientific skill they smashed our civilization and imprisoned or killed those highest in authority. Some died in the battle against them: others became sport for the Mithons and died that way—as I almost did in the arena. These

Mithons are a curious mixture of brilliant, inhuman skill—as far as science is concerned—and fiendish sadistic cruelty."

"The people we loosed from prison—the slaves we saw being conducted down a main street—were once all high dignitaries?" Abna questioned.

"Most of them. The situation is that the high dignitaries are put violently to death—while the others, who merely give open defiance but are not dignitaries, are used as slave workers in the Mithon factories. What the factories produce I have never been able to find out."

"You have no clue as to what the Mithons are trying to do?" the Amazon insisted.

"None whatever. They came from outer space, from a world of which we know nothing, and we stood no chance against them due to our lack of scientific knowledge. We have no conception of space travel. So far you four are the only ones to present serious opposition to the Mithons—and I warn you they will do their utmost to destroy you."

"Of that we're fully aware," the Amazon said grimly. "We have already had several narrow squeaks, and incidentally given the Mithons a run for their money. Our proposition now is to rejoin the battle. Agreed, Abna?"

"Definitely," Abna assented. "And it looks as if your guess about these bald-heads being from another world is right, Vi."

"Yes." She considered for a moment and then got to

her feet and paced around the control room, as was her habit when thinking. Stopping finally before the observation window, she looked down on the patchwork red of the planet.

"I think," the Amazon said slowly, "that we should return to the abode of the Supreme One. There we ought surely to find an explanation for his activities. Once we know that, we know what to attack. As it is, we'd be looking for a needle in a haystack."

"Return to his abode?" Abna repeated dubiously. "We wouldn't last five minutes! The miracle is that we've ever got this far."

The Amazon smiled as she came back to the table. "We shall not go as ourselves. I was thinking of microcosmosis."

"What is that?" Jalen asked in wonder.

"With the knowledge of science we have transferred to you, you may understand it," the Amazon said. "Microcosmosis is the art of reduction to infinite smallness—the narrowing of electronic orbits to produce microscopic smallness. If they are enlarged we get giantism. You understand?"

Jalen nodded, even though she looked rather surprised that she understood.

"But actual mass-weight remains the same?"

"No," the Amazon smiled, "at least, not with the process we use. Were that to remain the same, any reduced object would become immensely heavy, relative to its tiny size. A mass such as the *Ultra*, reduced to a pinpoint, would probably sink straight through the ground to the core of the planet!"

"Then how—?"

"The energy we use to compress electronic orbits also has anti-gravity properties, which has the effect of reducing the weight of the treated object exactly proportionate to the rate of shrinkage," the Amazon explained. "And when the object is returned to normal size, this energy is dissipated and normal mass-weight ratio is restored. On various occasions in our wanderings we have had need to use microcosmosis to further our plans, and I suggest that we should use it again. Reduce the *Ultra* and ourselves to pinpoint size and, while in that condition, see what we can discover. You agree, Abna?"

"Yes—I agree," he said slowly. "But there will be obstacles. In small size we may not be able to apprehend things in their right perspective."

"There is no other way to penetrate the Supreme One's abode and try and learn his secrets," the Amazon said. "Flaws there may be in the scheme, but it's the only way."

"All right," Abna agreed. "Let's try it.…"

He moved over to the electronic-reducing apparatus, and then glanced towards Jalen. She was looking worried, yet trying hard not to show it.

"There's nothing to fear, Jalen," Abna reassured her. "You will feel nothing, and see nothing, since everything in the ship—and the ship itself—will decrease in the same ratio. The only change will be in the apparent size of your planet and surroundings. Now—are we ready?"

Heads nodded, and after setting the amazing apparatus, Abna threw the switch. Immediately the *Ultra* and everything within it was gripped by a field of force. Except for a curiously tight feeling in the limbs and organs there was no change to those inside the ship— but all save Jalen, having experienced the sensation before—knew that every electronic orbit within their bodies was contracting, with the corresponding reduction in size, while the force field's anti-gravity properties automatically compensated for the increased weight in the reduction process.

* * * * * * *

The hundred miles back to Dard was soon accomplished, and thereafter Abna spent a considerable time trying to decide where to land. He finally chose a titanic red plain, and very slowly settled the *Ultra* down between two towering ridges. Then he switched off the power.

"As far as I can tell," he said slowly, as the others glanced al him, "we're on the roof of the Supreme One's abode. It's difficult to assess things with giantism all around us." He surveyed outside and then nodded. "Yes, I'm sure I'm right.… These red ridges, by the way, are ripples in the red surface of the roof. However.…" He broke off and patted the gun in his belt. "We're ready to explore."

"Here's a gun for you, Jalen," the Amazon said, handing her a holstered weapon attached to a belt.

"You've already proved you know how to fire it. Since this is your home planet, you may as well join us in fighting for its liberty."

"This time," Abna said, "I'm leaving the automatic control on the repulsive screen. It'll operate five minutes after we have left the ship. That, and the closed airlock, ought to seal it off from any prowlers, though they'd have to reduce to microscopic proportions to do anything."

"And what will happen when we return?" Jalen asked. "How will you get past the repulsive barrier?"

Abna pulled an instrument from his belt and tapped it. It looked somewhat like a complicated watch.

"This device is the answer, Jalen. Knowing the composition of the barrier, it's easy to devise a way of neutralizing it—at least within a given area. This instrument makes a space wide enough for the airlock to be opened from the outside by use of a hidden switch. After that, the rest is simple."

The girl of Dard smiled a little, wonder still deep in her blue eyes.

"You know every scientific trick, don't you?"

"And yet there is still much to learn," Abna said, putting the instrument back in his belt. "Probably these Mithons know a trick or two which will be new to us, and vice versa. The fact that we caught them trying to copy our power plant shows there is something there they don't know, and at a rough guess I'd say it is the secret of atomic power, by which the *Ultra* is driven."

The Amazon looked surprised. "Are you suggesting,

Abna, that a race as advanced as the Mithons actually don't know the secret of nuclear power?"

"I think it's possible. They've shown no evidence of it yet. They obviously understand spatial control to a high degree—as witness what happened to us in space, and also their golden ray stunt on the lavender planet. But nowhere have we seen a sign of nuclear power. If they had that, they would need far less power for everything they do.... Obviously they understand space travel, bnt I'd like to gamble it isn't done by atomic processes. Maybe these utilize magnetic lines of force; certainly something spatial again, in which art they seem to be masters."

And without any further elaboration of this rather surprising aspect of the situation, Abna set the automatic switches, then turned to the airlock and opened it. Silent, the others followed him outside, after which the airlock closed behind them. When they were some forty yards from the *Ultra* a mauve glory abruptly encased it—the repulsive screen.

"That's that," Abna commented significantly. "Now let's see where we are."

A strong leap against the lesser gravity carried him to the top of the mountain range that was the parapet, then he quickly uncoiled his nylon rope and tossed it down for the others to leap up and catch hold of. There was no difficulty except with Jalen. She, born and bred on the planet, had long since adapted herself to its gravity, therefore it was not in her favor. It took Viona and the Amazon a good ten minutes to haul her on to the parapet; then as she looked over the opposite side she reeled with giddiness.

Even normally the height from the Supreme One's abode to the depths of the city was in the region of 1,000 feet; but now that size and magnitude was magnified hundreds of times—which produced nothing but a blurred abyss of red, with the front of the Supreme One's abode sweeping down as an almost sheer cliff into the depths.

"Too much for you?" Abna asked, smiling, as he tossed his rope down the opposite side.

"I'll never make it," Jalen whispered. "It's—awful."

"We'll look after you," the Amazon said promptly. "Sit on my back, and hang on for your life. You'll be safe with me.... And is the rope long enough, Abna?"

He peered into the depths and presently shook his head.

"Not long enough by any means. Knot all our four ropes together."

This was duly done, the rope secured by hooks on the underledge of the parapet. During the process Jalen settled herself firmly on the Amazon's muscular back—but it was Abna who made the first descent into the depths. And depths they were indeed, his outlook not even comparable with that of a fly, so small was he.

The journey seemed appallingly long, with nothing but red void beneath him, but finally he beheld a sudden end to the 'cliff face' he was descending—an end in the shape of a gigantic opening, which could only be the open doorway of the Supreme One's abode.

He dropped from the rope—which was only just long enough—and tugged it twice to signify his safe arrival, then he stood waiting while the others descended. As he did so he smiled to himself at the comparison in sizes. Even the rope would appear far less thick than a hair to a normal person, and certainly would not be worthy of attention if perhaps the Supreme One, or a guard, happened to notice it dangling at one side of the entrance way.

Then, one by one, the others arrived. They stood surveying a gigantic cavern that was the hallway—while in the opposite directions at a considerable distance, there toiled gigantic men and machines, at work on repairing the wrecked bridge.

"I still can't understand why the Supreme One didn't retaliate," Abna said, pondering. "Anyway, there it is. Let's see what we can find. We'll leave our rope where it is for a getaway."

He led the way into the hall, the Amazon, Jalen, Viona, and Mexone coming behind him, in that order, everyone of them with their guns ready. Cautiously they proceeded along the enormous vista, the irregularities in the flooring appearing like small mountains over which they had to scramble.

So finally they came into the big room where the Supreme One had first 'received' them. It was completely empty, the furniture towering up invincibly in all directions, and the fibers of the carpet forming a waist-high jungle through which they were compelled to wade.

"Try the machine room," Abna said, and after fifteen minutes of pushing through the jungle of carpet they reached the stupendous, upended rectangle that marked the door. That it was closed did not present any difficulty. They walked beneath it and so came into a wilderness of machines, rendered all the more confusing by reason of the giantism.

"What now?" the Amazon questioned, and for reply Abna nudged her.

"Look! The man himself!"

The Amazon gave a start of surprise. What she had taken for a nearby pillar was actually the leg of a man. In fact, there were two men, seeming to tower infinite miles overhead, and one of them was unquestionably the Supreme One. Apparently, he was engaged in conversation with his colleague, but the words simply formed slow, indistinct ripples in the air and made no sense whatever. This was one of the penalties of extreme smallness.

Immediately the Amazon pulled an instrument from her belt and carefully adjusted it. It whistled slightly like an oscillating radio, but not sufficiently to attract the giants' attention; then to the ears of the intently listening five there gradually came the Supreme One's words, clearly enunciated, but in his own language. The lag in time was completely corrected by the instrument the Amazon was using.

"I'd forgotten the language difficulty," Abna muttered. "This doesn't make us much better off."

Jalen signaled quickly for silence, listening attentively to the instrument. Then after a moment she smiled.

"Perhaps I can repay your kindness by acting as interpreter," she said. "He's talking in the language of Dard, which is usual. I'll speak a second or so behind his words so as to give you an exact word-for-word statement."

Obviously proud of the fact that she was, for the moment, the most important member of the party Jalen prepared herself for her task, listening intently. Then she began speaking, repeating the Supreme One's words—

"'While they were here they certainly created a good deal of trouble, killing the guards, and releasing prisoners, even destroying the bridge—. But at least they did not create any real damage, otherwise I would have had to act more promptly."

"I submit, Supreme One, that it was perhaps foolish to give them so much freedom."

The Supreme One sighed with regret and moved slowly. His foot came down like an avalanche a fraction from Jalen as she moved quickly away. Quietly he strolled to the end of the big machine room and stood looking thoughtfully out of the window. After a moment or so his colleague joined him, all unaware that five anxious people had a route march to pursue in order to make contact again.

"I would suggest, Supreme One, that you forget the brief interlude of the cosmic wanderers.... Treat it as though it had never been and concentrate on the experiment. After all, that is really all that counts."

"Ah, yes—the experiment." The Supreme One brooded. "At times I grow rather weary of it, because the results are not what we want."

"Nonetheless, Supreme One, the motive behind our experiments makes it essential we should go on. Think of it! A race of mighty warriors—a whole planet full of them—and not one of them a natural being. A synthetic army to he launched against the worlds that surround us. A synthetic army to deal with the relentless powers that will sooner or later attack us."

"True," the Supreme One acknowledged, nodding his head slowly. "Yet despite the gift of a world supplied with chemicals which we can activate into life, we get the wrong results. That is what infuriates and wearies me! Instead of getting young people, lusty and full of power—we get old ones. Very old ones. We have tried to improve it by reversing the time law on the experimental world, but while it produces youth after age—in direct contradiction to Nature—the process becomes too swift when youth is reached, and babyhood almost immediately follows. If only we could create young people, then we could remove the time-reversal from the experimental world!"

"Perhaps we will in time," the other said, thinking.

Long silence, and five people of pinpoint size waiting tensely for his words. They had already learned far more than they had ever dared hope.

"I think," the Supreme One's colleague said presently, "That you would be well advised to increase the guard over our central power plant. If there is a revolution—and the possibility always exists—the insurgents have only to strike at the power plant to put everything out of action. The time-reversal, the spatial wave control—and the synthesis. The lot would stop. And I don't have to remind you that to recreate the power plant would take years. even as it took years to build it."

"I will give the matter my consideration," the Supreme One responded, though without much enthusiasm. "And, my friend, we had better see how they are progressing with the rebuilding of the bridge. Left too long to themselves, the engineers are inclined to be lazy. Come—let us see how they progress."

The Supreme One turned from the window, and in a moment he and his colleague had strode purposefully from the machine-room. Somewhere within its depths the five eavesdroppers looked at one another.

"Good work, Jalen," the Amazon exclaimed, patting the girl's thin arm in congratulation. "That was the best bit of quick-fire interpretation I've ever seen. Without you, it would probably have taken us months to find out anything concrete."

"True enough," Abna agreed. "At last we know what these bald-headed demons are driving at. We can easily fill in the gaps for ourselves. Apparently their own world is threatened by foes, presumably on neighbor planets. Not having enough forces at their disposal, they have selected this particular region for their activities, using this world as their base. The lethal, lavender-scented world they use as the creative ground, taking advantage of its natural chemicals and forming them, by an electronic patterner, into synthetic beings.… Incidentally, although the air of the lavender planet is lethal to us after a time, it evidently doesn't affect the synthetic beings, unless there is allowance made in their structure for the poison."

"They are only absorbing the air for a brief period," the Amazon pointed out. "That may account for it. The moment they are created they are transferred to Umnol. They hardly have the time to become doped."

"That may be it," Abna admitted. "Jalen, do you happen to know where this powerhouse is?"

She shook her head. "I have no idea. Remember, I have been in captivity since the Mithons came, and I have had no chance to identity any of the thousands of new buildings they have erected."

"New buildings!" the Amazon said abruptly. "Abna, that might help ns. At least it will narrow down the search. The new ones must be detectable from the old. In fact, they are," she went on, thinking. "Remember the patchwork effect which this world presents from above? That must be caused by the new edifices being mixed with the old."

"Very probably," Jalen agreed. "The original buildings of the city—indeed the whole planet—were all red. So the new ones were made in the same color."

"Then our next move is to find a building which looks like a powerhouse," the Amazon said, quite decided.

"Which raises obstacles," Abna pointed out. "We

can't possibly detect a powerhouse in our present microscopic state—yet if we return to normal we'll be immediately detected."

The group pondered for a moment, then the Amazon snapped her fingers.

"I have it! Retain our present size until we have flown 100 or 200 miles into space—just for safety's sake. The Supreme One won't bother trying to detect us since he assumes we've departed. At our 200-mile limit we return to normal size and study the planet telescopically. We pick out the building which we think is the powerhouse—and a few others as standbys in case we're wrong—then we reduce again to our present size, enter the powerhouse, and sum up the best means of attacking it."

Abna thought the plan out and nodded slowly. "Good enough—but this time I think we'll improve our chances by driving the minimized *Ultra* straight into the powerhouse. Then we shall feel it is always handy in case of emergency."

The decision taken, it was immediately acted upon. By slow degrees the quintet retraced their way alone the humpy floor, under the closed door of the machine-room, and so at length they came to the yawning vastness of the exterior and their still hanging nylon rope.

"Our friends seem to be busy with the bridge," Abna commented, and as the others looked they beheld the towering giants of the bald-heads hard at work, the Supreme One and his colleague looking on.

"If it were not for the complications which might

ensue," Abna said slowly, "I'd do something to undo everything they have done so far. Just for nuisance value."

He came to the edge of an idea, and then abandoned it. There was no sense in putting everything into jeopardy.... So the return climb up the rope to the parapet began—easy once again for the four, who took advantage of the gravity, but a nearly impossible feat for Jalen. Finally, since she could not make the climb, they tied the rope around her waist and left Abna to haul her to the parapet. Once this was done, it was only a short time before they had passed through the *Ultra*'s repulsive screen, with the aid of Abna's special neutralizing instrument, and were in the control room.

The airlock closed and the power plant hummed. A mere speck of dust in the air by comparison with its surroundings, the *Ultra* shot into the void.

CHAPTER TEN
JALEN'S SACRIFICE

At 200 miles from Dard's surface, Abna put the *Ultra* into an orbit. Then there began the restoration to normal—only a matter of minutes and entirely pain-less—and the vastness of Dard contracted to its proper perspective. This done, the five stood looking down on the planet from the observation window. Half Dard was sunk into a misty twilight, and the remainder was the usual patchwork red.

"Night's coming," Abna said. "Better wait until the day again and take some rest."

"And set the alarm system," the Amazon added. "Though we imagine we're safe, I never underestimate the enemy."

So the alarm was set in operation and, after a meal, the five retired to rest. They slept well after their exertions, Jalen in particular, awakening some eight hours later to find Dard emerging from the shadow of night as she completed a revolution on her axis.

There followed breakfast, by which time the main center of Dard had emerged completely from the night. Careful telescopic observations began, the Amazon taking the first sitting at the eyepiece. Amid the vast huddle of buildings—even allowing for the fact that some were new and some old—her task was still not an easy one; until at length she singled out an edifice that seemed to offer promise, mainly on account of the fact that its roof bristled with curious antennae, added to the fact that the dim dots of guards prowling in constant watchfulness around the roof were visible. Under greater magnification this assumption became amply verified.

"It may well be it," the Amazon said, explaining the circumstances. "See what you think, Abna."

Abna nodded, drawing a rough sketch as he gazed through the window.

"I think we can get our direction all right," he said. "We have to remember that we're going to assume microcosmosis again, and that's going to alter our sense of values."

Abna had by no means an easy task with the surroundings so changed, but by following the sketch he had made, and mentally making allowances for the giantism, he did finally succeed in bringing the now-tiny vessel down on the enormous plain which was the roof of the hoped-for powerhouse. Immediately he cut off the power and moved to the window. With the others he stood gazing out on the red plain. Across it at intervals moved vast shapes—the legs of the men acting as guards, men who would not notice this speck of dirt which was actually one of the mightiest space ships ever created.

"Well, we're here," he said grimly, turning. "And from here on we'll probably have plenty of fun and games. Check your guns and make sure they are okay."

This was done, then when tabloid provisions had been packed and pocketed, Abna opened the airlock and stepped outside to the red plain with its hummocky surface. In silence the others followed him, accustomed by now to the fantastic giantism of everything.

Entry into the powerhouse was an easy task, since there were numbers of ventilators in the roof. It was simply a matter of climbing between the slats of the various orifices and then lowering themselves down with rope. By this process, which had all the ingredients of mountaineering, they managed not only to get inside the building, but also to climb down one of the roof pillars—and so to the central gangway between rows upon rows of throbbing generators.

The fact that they had evidently found the right place was offset somewhat by the enormity of the machines. Even had they been in their normal size the generators would have been massive, but as seen from pinpoint vantage they occupied all heaven and earth in a vast circle of humming, whirring metal, the lamps over them looking exactly like distant stars.

"I begin to wonder," Abna said seriously, "if your idea was such a good one, Vi. How do you propose dealing with machines this size?'"

The Amazon looked troubled. "Frankly, I don't know. And we have no means of knowing which one it would be best to wreck."

"There's one way of doing it," Mexone, who had obviously been thinking, commented. "Go back to the *Ultra*, get inside it, then fly around this powerhouse until we observe a vital-looking machine. Once we do, drop a nuclear bomb on it. The bomb will have effect—devastating effect, since its lesser size won't make it any the less efficient—yet the *Ultra* won't appear any bigger, if as big, than a full stop flying around."

"It's an idea," the Amazon agreed. "If we can—"

She stopped abruptly, her hand stealing to her gun as the stupendous shape of a man appeared near her. Then she started in consternation as she realized that the man's shape was slowly becoming smaller. So were the machines. The whole stupendous area of the powerhouse was closing in gradually.

"Abna, we're enlarging!" she exclaimed hoarsely, and made to clash away from the looming figure—but she was rooted to the floor with the old, familiar magnetism.

Then suddenly, the whole picture became clear as it was reduced to normal dimensions. Straining helplessly at the floor, their guns ready, the group stood staring at the unmistakable figure of the Supreme One. They tried to take aim with their weapons, but the magnetism in the floor prevented them from even raising their hands.

"Very interesting," the Supreme One commented, his eyes glinting. "Very interesting indeed. I rather wondered what you would do next, my friends. Ah, I observe you have Jalen Naisoom with you. I rather thought that would he the case."

"All right," Abna said coolly, "you win. What do you propose doing now?"

"Ridding myself of you finally and completely, when I have learned certain things. The main concern is the whereabouts of your *Ultra*. While instruments have kept track of you, and your various moves from large to small, they have not kept track of the *Ultra* due to its disturbing repulsive screen. That I must have at all costs."

"Then the story you told a colleague of yours that you thought we had left the planet was untrue?" Viona asked.

"Of course. I knew exactly where you were, and what you were doing—but I wanted to see your final moves. I was right in my guess that you would make for this powerhouse here.... Now, I will read from your minds where your ship is—"

"Blank your minds!" the Amazon said quickly. "Don't let him know a thing!"

The scarlet eyes smoldered in fury; then distended enormously. The battering ram of mental compulsion was at work again, probing and compelling an overpowering example of the lethal force of a superbly trained intelligence.... And yet it was not strong enough to break down the united opposition of four minds almost equally trained, and one extra one creating just enough disturbance to upset the balance.

The Supreme One relaxed suddenly, pondering. The five who opposed him relaxed a trifle and, perforce, waited.

"Evidently you are more intelligent than I had imagined," he commented. "Which in a sense makes you all the more dangerous. However, there is always the physical way."

Coming forward, he paused in front of Jalen—about a foot away, which was probably the fringe of the magnetism. The girl looked for a moment into his terrible eyes, then looked away again.

"You, of less intelligence and strength than these other four, can probably tell me what I want to know," the Supreme One said. "At least we will see."

He pulled a weapon from his belt and snapped it on, covering the girl in a flood of pink light. For a moment it seemed as though he was going to kill her, but this evidently was not his intention. The pink radiance simply acted as a neutralizer, making it possible for the girl to move.

"Come here!" the Supreme One commanded, and very slowly Jalen did as she was told. Some latent instinct prompted her to jerk up her gun, but the Supreme One anticipated her action. With one blow he knocked her six feet away, her gun clattering to the floor out of reach.

"You should know better than that, Jalen."

Nearly erupting with fury, yet unable to do anything about it, the quartet stood watching as Jalen slowly rose up, naked terror in her face as she faced the squat intellectual monster.

"Where," the Supreme One asked quietly, "is the

Ultra? You know, and you will tell me. Now!"

"I'll not.... I'll not tell you!" Jalen whispered straining with every ounce of her body and mind against mental compulsion.

"Yes, you will, Jalen. Because my mind is stronger than yours."

This was torture on the highest plane—the slow breaking down of Jalen's energy reserve until she became nothing else but a crushed, beaten slave willing to tell everything she knew. She knew the danger to herself, and the inevitability of it, as she rocked and swayed in anguish before the intellectual blast.

Then for an instant she must have had a flash of lucidity. She swung around, dropped her hands from her face, and dived for the gun that had been knocked out of her hand when she had been knocked down. Sheer desperation carried her through the tugging force of the Supreme One's mind, carried her to the point where she lifted the gun—but not at her torturer. Instead she turned it inwards, on herself, and with her last vestige of conscious action pressed the button.

The action came us such a horrifying surprise that even the Supreme One gazed in astonishment. There was the familiar intense flame, then gradually drifting smoke. The gun clattered down to the floor, leaving blank nothing where Jalen had been standing.

"The fool! The little fool!" the Amazon cried hoarsely. "Why did she have to do that?"

"To prevent herself giving any information, of course," Abna said slowly. "It was the only way she could think of—and it was the act of a heroine." He paused and looked at the Mithon ruler. "Well, Supreme One?" he asked coldly. "What are you going to do now? Jalen was a little too clever for you, wasn't she? And she was the only one who would have spoken. We never will."

"That remains to be seen," the Supreme One said. "Sooner or later one or other of you will forget yourself for a moment and allow the thought of the *Ultra* to come into your mind. In the meantime, it is no use leaving you standing there." And he released them with his pink beam.

"One thing I would ask," Abna said, after a moment. "Was the story related by yourself and your colleague—deliberately for our benefit—a true one? Or was it something improvised on the spur of the moment?"

"It was true," the Supreme One replied calmly. "We seek to create youthful synthetic beings on the world of Umnol, and because the mechanics of such a feat requires enormous slave labor, the people of this world have been pressed into service for our machines. They had some kind of government when we came, which we quickly destroyed. We are confident that in the end we shall create the youthful legions we desire, and so have a vast, inexhaustible army with which to demolish our enemies."

"Who surround your home planet?" Abna asked.

"Exactly."

"Basing my conclusions on what I have seen of the Mithon race," the Amazon said, "I would say that you do not fear your neighbors so much as that you are anxious to overpower them."

"I have no intention of discussing the matter at length," he said curtly. "Let us take some other aspect— some scientific angle in which we are both interested."

The Amazon seemed about to give another caustic answer, but Abna spoke first.

"We will admit one thing: we were nearly beaten by your attack on us in outer space. We assume you used spatial vibration?"

"Exactly so. Follow me...."

Still taking care to guard their thoughts, and alert, too, for the first sign of relaxed vigilance on the part of the Supreme One, the four followed him to a complex mass of machinery in another quarter of the power-house. He indicated its humming, whirring enormity.

"This is the heart and center of spatial vibration," he said. "Power is generated here to the machine-rooms, and in turn the machine-rooms produce the necessary process of creating backward time on the world of Umnol, in the hope that we may force our synthetic creations into a period of youthfulness—and there maintain them. The critical task is getting the maintenance of youth. So far we have not been successful."

"How do you create the backward time illusion?" the Amazon asked bluntly. "The reversing of all emotions, so that love becomes hate, and so forth?"

"The reversal of the emotions is purely a natural consequence of the reversed state of time—an offshoot. It serves its purpose in that it creates a cold individuality that does not need or desire friendship. Such types are always best for conquest.... As to the process: I know you understand the laws governing the probability of the electron, so you will understand me when I say this is a modification of the theory. Stated briefly, space and time are interlocked. You cannot move in time without moving in space; nor can you move in space without moving in time. Space is not really space, as you are aware. It is a series of vibrations—a vast agglomeration of them—that go under the heading of space-time. In this particular space, this universe, the fusing of the various vibrations that create space and matter are far more obvious than the space from which you came. You come from a different space and universe: that I know from your minds."

"Yes, that is so," the Amazon agreed. "Maybe that is why in our attempts to get spatial vibration we haven't succeeded. Our highest achievement in this line is limited to radio, television, and such like, which are basically mere ripples in the fabric of space."

"Your space is less—so to speak—solid than ours," the Supreme One explained. "With the right equipment we can handle it as solidly as though it were matter. In the normal course of events it all flows one way, moving in a perpetual circle, like the rim of a wheel around a central hub. That is normal time and space. But if a section of it is compelled to flow the opposite way, space is, so to speak, turned back on itself and everything in that space. In other words, Time is compelled to reverse because space is reversed. The two conditions are never separate. That is what is done. The space around Umnol is reversed, producing the state of backward Time.... Just as if you had a bowl of water with an object floating in the water, it would go one way if you agitated the water into a whirlpool; but you could easily make it go backwards by agitating the whirlpool in the opposite direction. You understand?"

"Perfectly," the Amazon assented. "And presumably, with the reversal of Time, everything within the area is affected in the same way."

"That is correct," the Supreme One agreed, "and in regard to our attacking your machine in space, the process was only slightly different. Once we had located you, the only necessity was for us to send forth a ripple in space, with its main apex converging on your space ship."

"And power?" Abna asked. "What do you use for that? You must need enormous energy."

"We do—hence my wish to learn from you the secret of nuclear energy." There was a grim silence for a moment and then the Supreme One added: "We use the energy of the sun—the greatest known source in the light of our present science."

The Amazon strolled around the machinery, inspecting it in genuine interest. Then presently she asked another question.

"Is it also another peculiarity of your space that enables you to walk through solid walls?"

"Purely the application of the fourth dimension, which when you understand it enables its application by a sheer effort of mind. Under that effort the inter-stices of space are made to part sufficiently for a body to pass through—hence, through a wall. It demands enormous concentration, and the effect is only fleeting, but effective."

"How," Viona asked, in the following silence, "do you go about the creation of beings on the—the scented, in-between world?"

"I have no reason to explain anything further to you," the Supreme One snapped, obviously a bit discomfited that he had been carried away to explain so much already.

"We have a system of our own," the Amazon put in. "Many times in the past we have created synthetic beings—even duplicated ourselves—by means of a Patterner."

The Supreme One was silent, obviously annoyed to discover that the four were not very far behind him in knowledge. Indeed, they were probably equal. The differences in knowledge lay in the fact that different spaces, different universes, were involved—each peculiar to its own construction.

"Manifestly we know atomic science intimately—and the art of contraction and expansion," Abna said. "How otherwise do you suppose we contracted ourselves to extreme smallness in order to invade your domain?"

"Yet my knowledge of that science must be equal with yours by reason of the fact that I forced you to normal size," the Supreme One retorted. "And with that very machine!"

He pointed to a mass of equipment close by. The four looked towards it quickly.

"Very similar to ours," the Amazon said, going closer to study the details. Under the pretence of studying the machine earnestly—which indeed she was doing to discover how it operated—the Amazon also watched her opportunity. It came when the Supreme One turned from watching her to say something to Abna. Instantly she acted.

Quick as an arrow under the light gravity she hurled herself forward and brought the powerful Mithon to the floor in an amazing flying tackle. He struggled violently, taken by surprise—but for all his iron strength the Amazon was ready for him. She dealt blow after blow with hammer viciousness, on the back of his thick neck just below the edge of the skull bone until he was still.

Smiling grimly to herself, the Amazon rose up and looked at the others.

"Why this?" Abna asked, puzzled. "It won't get us anywhere. Why not kill him and have done with it?"

"I don't want to kill him—yet. There are countless others like him on this planet who'll carry on where he left off. No, I've a much better plan that that. A plan which will also make him suffer for all the things he's done to the poor wretches on Umnol, to say nothing of avenging poor Jalen."

She went across to the Electron Controller.

"We're contracting!" Viona exclaimed. "Becoming

smaller! But why?"

"So we can return to the *Ultra*, of course. We could never have done so otherwise. Thanks to the Supreme One telling us so much, I found out how to escape back to smallness—"

There followed more long moments of anxious waiting—and still more contraction. The Amazon was clearly growing more worried than was usual.

"We must pull this trick before the Supreme One recovers," she explained, as Abna looked at her inquiringly. "Otherwise he might be able to save himself. When I say so, run."

Since her remarks did not make sense, Abna let the subject drop—but he grabbed Viona and Mexone by the arm and started to run as the Amazon gave a shout. They kept going for a while along the vast plain of the center aisle-way, then at length the Amazon slowed to a stop, looking back at the gigantic motionless hill which represented the Supreme One's still unconscious body.

"So far, so good," the Amazon said, breathing hard. "Now come on—back to the *Ultra*."

As fast as possible they completed their journey to the ship and thankfully entered the control room. The airlock closed—then in the bright light Abna looked at the Amazon curiously.

"If you don't mind, Vi, I'd like an explanation. What are we going to do?"

"Win our battle," the Amazon said simply, and pulling forward the power lever she set the *Ultra* on the move.

CHAPTER ELEVEN
DEATH OF THE MITHONS

Since the situation was now manifestly in the hands of the Amazon, there was nothing the others could do except watch. They moved to the window and gazed outside on the vast wilderness of the powerhouse: then it became apparent to them that they were moving gradually toward the mountainous body of the Supreme One as he still lay unconscious on the floor.

"Where are we going?" Viona asked, astonished. "We'll collide with him in a moment."

"No, we won't." The Amazon shook her head and indicated what looked to be a curiously shaped cave ahead. "That's where we're going—right inside."

Abna gave a start. "But that's the Supreme One's ear!'"

"Exactly. To us in our reduced state it appears like a cave mouth. I intend that we shall enter his skull, and after that find a landing point somewhere. I imagine the interior will, to us, look like any cave, and the kind of ledge we'll need will actually be bone or tissue structure. Once we have found a resting place, we're in a perfect position to influence that dominant, diabolical brain of his."

The immensity and incredibility of the scheme held the others silent. Awestruck, they watched as the *Ultra*—tiny beyond conceiving—swept into the vastness of the dark that was actually the Supreme One's ear. Then there was darkness, the darkness of the interior of his skull.

The Amazon switched on the powerful searchlight, and the illumination cast upon what looked like the gray walls of a monstrous cavern. Any resemblance between the interior of a head and the gigantic vastness of ledges and ridges of gray was prevented by the different scales of size.

"There!" the Amazon said abruptly, pointing ahead to a ridge clearly illumined in the blaze. "That's an excellent resting place."

She moved to the controls and maneuvered the vessel gently until finally it came to rest. She viewed the scene outside for a moment, and then switched off the searchlight.

"Now for action," she said grimly. "We have thought-amplifying equipment, but we've never had a chance to use it against the Supreme One. This time we're going to."

"We've done a few strange things," Abna reflected. "But I think this one is the most extraordinary.... Mass hypnosis from within the skull!"

"Exactly," the Amazon assented, moving to the Thought Amplifier and adjusting its controls. "And here is the subject of our concentration: We shall command the Supreme One, when he recovers consciousness, to order every one of his fellow Mithons to the powerhouse. Every single one of them, wherever they may be!"

"And what then?" Abna inquired.

"They will be destroyed," the Amazon shrugged. "A destructive killer-race of this world will be utterly destroyed. Jalen, too, will be avenged. The people of this world will resume their normal way of life, and the synthetic people of Umnol will find time has become normal. They in time will react naturally and a race will begin."

"You're a bit ahead of yourself," Abna said. "The time on Umnol will become normal, you say. How? That demands destruction of all the machinery in this powerhouse. Even the death of the master-race won't stop the machinery functioning for a long time to come."

"This powerhouse will be destroyed, with the race," the Amazon said.

She adjusted the Thought Amplifier controls to her satisfaction and then looked up earnestly.

"As I said before, all of us have one concentration," she said deliberately. "That one concentrated thought is: call all Mithons to the powerhouse. Now— we concentrate on that to the exclusion of everything else. Three minutes of unwavering thought command should be sufficient."

The four moved into a close circle to be as close as possible to the instrument's transmitting plate.

This done, the Amazon reached out and snapped off the repulsive screen from around the *Ultra*, then she switched on the Thought Amplifier. There was silence, except for the faint hum of the apparatus in action. And, invisibly, there spread from the *Ultra* a series of concentric waves, each one of them reaching and being absorbed by the Supreme One's brain.

The Supreme One began moving, bewildered, yet knowing he must obey this mysterious impulse. He went with deliberate steps to the general broadcasting equipment and switched it on. In another moment his voice was booming through the gigantic city.

"Summoning all members of the Mithon race to the Central Powerhouse. The Supreme One commands it and it must be instantly obeyed, no matter what else is occupying your attention. Summoning all members...."

Then, gradually, a new thought took possession of him, almost as amazing as its predecessor, and before he could find no way of circumventing it. Yet again he went to the radio and switched it on.

"You are commanded to listen to the Supreme One, wherever you may be! All except the members of the Mithon race, who have already received their orders, will immediately retreat from regions near the Central Powerhouse, and will give it isolation of at least twelve miles. Evacuation to bring this order into effect will begin at once, or else I shall not be responsible for the consequences. Those who hear this order will immediately pass it on to anybody who has not heard it. That is all."

Again the Supreme One switched off, his bewilderment increasing. He knew that the orders were hypnotic, and the mystery was that he could not fight against the influence.

Then the first of his followers arrived—to be followed almost immediately by another, until they began arriving in dozens from all parts of the planet, the more distant ones having taken the first and fastest means of travel to obey the command.

For an hour they kept coming, until a roll call revealed that every man was present. Only then did the Supreme One cross to the huge doors of the power-house and close them. Slowly he turned to face the waiting assembly. They looked back at him, then at one another, at a loss to account for the vacant look on the Supreme One's face, the tight-drawn lines of pain about his mouth.

And within the *Ultra* four more people were also somewhat mystified. They had no means of knowing exactly what was happening: they did not know if the hypnotic orders they had issued had had any effect.

"Well, what now?" Abna asked presently. "Do you suppose he's done what he was told to do?"

The Amazon started from a spell of thought. "We can't leave this business in doubt, not knowing whether we're getting any results or not," she said. "We might try short-range television and see what it gets us."

Since the transmission-reception was taking place from within the Supreme One's skull—quite painlessly—there was no sign of the Supreme One on the screen. Instead the men grouped around him were clearly visible, most of them looking tense, and quite a few were horrified. In the background another man was making adjustment to an instrument not unlike a photographic enlarger.

"From the look of things," the Amazon said, studying the screen intently, "the first part of our plan seems to have worked all right. The power-house doors are closed for one thing, and for another I should think the numbers of Mithons present constitutes all there are of them. My plan is to enlarge the *Ultra* and so eventually kill the Supreme One, and when he explodes, blow up the powerhouse itself."

"So that was your idea!" Viona glanced sharply. "That was why you wanted all Mithons in the power-house? To wipe out the lot?"

"Just a moment," Mexone said, as the Amazon moved to the switchboard. "Granted that enlargement would completely annihilate the Supreme One—but why should there be an explosion?"

"Because two bodies are trying to occupy the same space at the same time," the Amazon answered, closing the switches on the Electronic Contractor. "The shock waves alone will cause an explosion, apart from the actual enlargement."

Grim-faced, the Amazon kept the electronic machine on full power far beyond the normal limit needed for enlargement to actual size. Until at last there was a sudden shock and the *Ultra* quivered. Only then did she cut out the apparatus.

"We are now somewhere in the region of thirty feet tall," she said grimly, "and the *Ultra* is correspondingly increased in size. What damage have we done?"

"Plenty, by the look of it," Viona said, at the observation window with Mexone.

The Amazon and Abna looked for themselves—and the view was certainly amazing. The *Ultra* stood motionless amid a litter of twisted metal girders. In all directions, looking quite small by reason of the *Ultra*'s giantism, sprawled the city—but for a distance of perhaps a mile, in. varying degrees of destruction, everything had been razed to the ground.

"Well," said Abna, "We've destroyed all the Mithons and the machine at one blow! This world and Umnol can deal with matters for themselves from now on. Our job's finished."

Satisfied, the Amazon returned the *Ultra* to its normal size. "We'll take one look at Umnol and check on it before we depart," the Amazon said; and with a nod Abna set the course in the planet's direction.

In a very short time they had reached it, skimming over the forests. It was in the course of this that Abna slowed the vessel almost to a halt so that observations could be made. And the observations were conclusive.

"Okay," the Amazon said, with a satisfied smile. "The trees are growing normally and not backwards. That's all we need to know. Time has restored itself and Disi and his people will be feeling the benefit."

"Do we need to see him?" Viona asked, and the Amazon shook her head.

"No, we've finished our task. Let's go home."

Abna grinned as he set the *Ultra* moving upwards again with rising velocity.

"Even in our own space, home is the deuce of a long way from the Milky Way!"

The Amazon said nothing. For a long time she stood watching the world of Umnol receding into distance. Finally the entire system with its brilliant sun was only a smudge in the firmament and there was nothing but the unfamiliar Universe on all sides.

"I think we're ready for the switch back into our own space," Abna said, locking the controls. "Let's move." He hurried from the control room to the compartment where the Probability Machine stood. Since the machine was already set from the previous operation, he had only to put it into reverse and then set a five-minute time limit switch. This done, he came back into the control room.

"Right," he said. "Get on the pressure beds."

The Amazon, Viona, and Mexone promptly obeyed, and then lay watching the chronometer as it clicked off the decreasing seconds. As the fourth minute began to fade away they tensed a little for the anguish to come—and precisely on the fifth minute it came, the same torturing experience as before. They felt again the twisting of body, nerve, and mentality into strain and stress as one space gave way to another. Then gradually the feeling abated and they slowly returned to normal.

The moment they got off the pressure beds they

hurried to the window, where Abna was already standing. He was looking puzzled—and the others, too, felt a growing sense of bewilderment.

There was not a star in sight!

"Where—where are we?" Viona stammered, turning amazed eyes to her father.

"Quite truthfully, I don't know." He glanced at the displays on the switch-panel. "We're moving at close on the velocity of light relative to a fixed point, and we should have re-entered our own space in a position close to the Milky Way.… Yet space is dark, despite the terrific speed at which we're passing though it."

For nearly five minutes they stood there, staring through the non-reflective glass on to the abyss. They kept telling themselves that stars, or a light, must appear soon. But none did.

Finally the Amazon could stand it no longer. She raced to the Probability Machine chamber and checked the instrument's readings. There was no mistake: everything was in order. She turned a thoughtful face as Abna, Viona, and Mexone joined her.

"We've undoubtedly come into our space, yet nothing is visible," she said slowly. "Why? Unless.…" A thought seemed to strike her. "Wait a moment!"

She hurried back into the control room and went straight to the computer console, where she busied herself with equations—for nearly half an hour. Not even Abna dared interrupt her. Finally she switched off and looked up at Abna.

"Well?" he asked quietly. "Do you know the answer?"

"Yes, I do. We've come into our own space all right, but by some misfortune we've emerged in the Coal sack, that dark emptiness in the Milky way near the Southern Cross. No astronomer has ever yet explained what the Coal sack—or other similar vacuities—really comprises. We don't know its depth, even though we know its width."

The others became silent and looked at one another. Then they moved to the window. To reverse the ship would take a long time, and even then they would not be sure of being on the right course. They were in void, in every meaning of the word.

"We shall—just have to carry on," Viona said at length.

"Yes," Abna agreed. "Although the Probability Machine was right, we overlooked the movement of the Milky Way itself in the time we were absent."

"It must end somewhere," the Amazon mused, slowly taking heart again. "And we'll go toward that end as long as our power holds out!"

ABOUT THE AUTHOR

British writer JOHN RUSSELL FEARN was born near Manchester, England, in 1908. As a child he devoured the science fiction of Wells and Verne, and was a voracious reader of the Boys' Story Papers. He was also fascinated by the cinema, and first broke into print in 1931 with a series of articles in *Film Weekly*.

He then quickly sold his first novel, *The Intelligence Gigantic*, to the American magazine, *Amazing Stories*. Over the next fifteen years, writing under several pseudonyms, Fearn became one of the most prolific contributors to all of the leading US science fiction pulps, including such legendary publications as *Astounding Stories*, *Startling Stories*, *Thrilling Wonder Stories*, and *Weird Tales*.

During the late 1940s he diversified into writing novels for the UK market, and also created his famous superwoman character, The Golden Amazon, for the prestigious Canadian magazine, the Toronto *Star Weekly*. In the early 1950s in the UK, his fifty-two novels as "Vargo Statten" were bestsellers, most notably his novelization of the film, *Creature from the Black Lagoon*.

Apart from science fiction, he had equal success with westerns, romances, and detective fiction, writing an amazing total of 180 novels—most of them in a period of just ten years—before his early death in 1960. His work has been translated into nine languages, and continues to be reprinted and read worldwide.

www.ingramcontent.com/pod-product-compliance
Lightning Source LLC
Chambersburg PA
CBHW050754250626
47155CB00005B/2060